"Thor, Baldacci, Flynn, Hamburg. Get ready as Banner fits right in!"

"Move over Jack Reacher there's a new guy taking over."

"Great stuff. Exciting and fast paced. On par with Flynn & Thor."

"The writing was superior, the story line was compelling and the action was top-notch. Sorry I could only give this one a five star rating!"

THE CELL

A HARRY BAUER THRILLER

BLAKE BANNER

R

RIGHTHOUSE

ISBN-13: 978-1-63696-417-1

ISBN-10: 1-63696-417-6

Cover design by: Damonza

Printed in the United States of America

www.righthouse.com

www.instagram.com/righthousebooks

www.facebook.com/righthousebooks

twitter.com/righthousebooks

HARRY BAUER THRILLER SERIES

ONE

I HAVE LIVED HAUNTED BY THE VISION OF A CHILD'S eyes.

I am not a religious man. I believe in reality. Maybe there is a greater truth back of that reality, underlying it. I don't know. I don't think anybody does. But one thing I am sure of is that the path to that truth, if it exists, does not involve hating and sentencing to death all those who stray from your idea of what is right.

That child could not have been more than four or five years old. She was pretty with very black hair and dark eyes. She was one of the people massacred at Al-Landy, where, in the name of God, in the name of what was right according to their religion, every man, woman, and child was murdered after being tortured, raped, or both. Their crime had been a crime against God. Their crime was wanting to buy a TV for the village café, and that constituted blasphemy, a denial of God.

I was there with my patrol, hidden in the sand dunes above the village, and I watched it happen. I watched them through the scope on my C8 Carbine. I watched them drive in in their trucks with their guns. I watched them round up the village. Somehow my eyes had locked on to that little girl's eyes, and her fear and grief was burned into my mind. I never knew her name. I never knew her parents or her family. All I knew was her terror, her pain, and her deep sadness. They became a part of me, a part of what I had become.

A killer.

I don't do therapy. I don't think there are many people in this world who would know how to heal the massacre at Al-Landy. But a few months back, I ran into an old friend, Sam Jorgensen, who had spent several years with Delta Force and had seen his fair share of the darkness human beings are capable of creating. When he retired, he'd devoted his life to studying the human mind and got doctorates in psychology and philosophy. We'd gotten drunk together, and I'd told him about Al-Landy and the fact that I had hunted down the man responsible for the massacre, Mohammed Ben Amini, and I had killed him. But the little girl's eyes still haunted me.

He had told me to bury her. To find a place that was peaceful and quiet, undisturbed by human madness, to take something that represented her and bury it in that place and give her peace. A place where her soul could be at peace.

It took me seven months to build up the courage, but I'd finally decided to get the rifle and the scope through which I had watched the massacre, take them up to the Wind River Mountains in Wyoming, as high as I could climb, to those places where, when you look down, you feel your soul could take off and fly, and there bury that child, give her soul peace and, if there is a God of Love and Forgiveness, commit her soul to that god's care.

I had wrapped my C8 Carbine and scope in black silk and placed them in a wooden box. Then I had climbed into my Grenadier truck outside my old brownstone on James Baldwin Place and driven the two thousand plus miles to Pinedale. It took me all of thirty-four hours because I stopped on the way at a motel for a few hours' sleep.

Once in Pinedale, I stopped again, briefly, at my house on Pole Creek Road. There I showered, had coffee, and grabbed a bottle of whiskey. Then I drove to the Sacred Rim trailhead. From there, I walked for a couple of hours into the mountains, carrying the boxed C8 Carbine and scope on my back, past Photographer's Point to a place where Freemont Creek tumbles out of the Winds into a deep canyon on its journey toward Freemont Lake. The view from there cannot be described with words, but it always seems to me to defy gravity and makes you believe that perhaps, after all, we have a soul, and that soul can rise above the hell that is this world and fly.

It was while I sat there with these rare thoughts, mourning a child I never had, whose name I did not even know, mourning the childhood she might have had, the happiness she might have had, and the existence I myself might have had— devoted to life instead of death—it was while I was mourning that child and preparing to lay her to rest that my phone rang.

There is no signal at that height in the Wind River Moun- tains. Phones don't work up there. Which meant the call could have come from just one person.

I closed my eyes, swore as one is not supposed to swear at a funeral, decided firmly not to answer it, and put it to my ear.

"Sir?"

The brigadier's clipped English voice answered. "Harry, are you in New York?"

"No."

"How soon can you get back? It's urgent."

I sighed quietly. "I'll leave my truck here and get a plane. Give me maybe six or seven hours."

There was a frown in his voice. "Where are you?"

I hesitated a fraction of a second. "Pinedale."

"Oh. Claire?"

"No. I'm up in the mountains."

"I see. I'm sorry to interrupt. It's important. You'll see when you get here. What's your nearest airport? Ralph Wenz, isn't it?"

"Yeah."

"That's a little less than two thousand miles. I'll send the company plane. Give him three or four hours. I'll call you when he's about to touch down."

"You're sending the plane? It's that important?"

"Yes. That important."

"OK, I'm on my way."

I said it without enthusiasm, hung up, sighed deeply, and looked up into the vast blue dome of the sky. I spoke across time to someplace outside of space where I wanted to believe she could hear me.

"I'll come back," I said. "I'll set you free." And as I spoke, a name came to me. A name that made me smile. I shrugged, and after a moment I added, "Miriam." She'd looked like a Miriam, I decided.

I made my way back through the pinewoods to the trail-head. There I packed the stuff carefully in the truck, and on the drive back to my house on Pole Creek Road, as the sun blazed across the western horizon, I wondered what was so important that the brigadier would send Cobra's specially adapted long haul Gulfstream to get me back to New York in the shortest time modern technology would allow. Israel, Iran, Syria, Ukraine, and North Korea all passed through my mind, but they were not my department. There were other agencies that took care of international crises of that sort. I was strictly a hit man—and a semi-retired one at that. I'd be fully retired, I told myself as I pulled up outside my house, if they'd let me.

———

I SLEPT through the flight and touched down in Teterboro just after midnight. There was a Grand Cherokee waiting for me with a driver in a blue suit who might have been an android with limited artificial intelligence. He asked me if I was me, and when I told him I was, he carried my bag to the Jeep and drove me, through the sleeping darkness of suburban street lamps, to the Cobra headquarters one and a half miles north of Pleasantville.

There, after going through the elaborate security of facial recognition and voice recognition, I was led across a checkerboard floor to the library, where I found the brigadier seated in his chesterfield in front of the fire. He stood as I was shown in and approached me with both hands outstretched.

"Harry, good of you to come at such short notice. Have you eaten? Will you have a drink?"

I told him I was fine, but he ignored me and poured us a whiskey each anyway. He sat as he handed me my drink and sighed.

"This is a unique situation, Harry. I am aware you are in need of time to think about your future and whether you want to continue as an operative with Cobra or not, and I would not, under any other circumstances, have troubled you."

I sipped my drink and set it down on the table beside me.

"You don't normally talk around a subject either, sir. I'm here. What's it about?"

He took another deep breath. "Cobra is not officially sanctioned, as you know. However, within that, we operate under tight rules, and we are very careful about how we select our targets, and we have very strict criteria."

"Crimes against humanity."

"Quite, and that is strictly defined. As you know, we are very careful to avoid a culture of just picking off anyone who gets on some Western leader's nerves. The risk is there and constant, and we guard against it."

I nodded, smiled, and spread my hands. "So...?"

"There is an exception to every rule, and that exception has cropped up with a vengeance, if you will forgive the expression."

I arched an eyebrow at him. "An exception? What kind of an exception?"

"Before I tell you, let me just say this. You will be briefed, and if you decide you don't want to do the job, you will be flown back to Pinedale, or wherever you want to go, and the case will be closed and shelved. You understand that? You are the only operative I know of to whom I would entrust this job."

"I'm flattered. What is the job?"

"You have heard of Jeff Cook."

It wasn't a question, but I said, "Yes, of course. The founder of the Clearwater Corporation. He's a tech giant, defense contractor..." I frowned, unaware of his involvement in any kind of crime against humanity. "Is he the target?"

"No. I am not sure if you are aware of it, but his wife was killed in a traffic accident a couple of years ago. They had one daughter, Beverly. She was twelve at the time of her mother's death. She and her father live together at Clearlake, about an hour's drive north of San Francisco. As you can imagine, after the mother's death, she and her father became very close. She is home schooled..." He trailed off, making circular 'on and on' motions with his hand that somehow suggested she and her dad hung out together a lot. I hazarded a guess.

"Jeff Cook is a friend of yours."

"Yes. We have been friends for some time."

He watched me. I drew breath and picked up my drink. "You said this is a job you would only entrust to me, and you've made a point of mentioning his daughter. She is what, fourteen now?"

"Yes."

"I am guessing this involves the child, and that is why you want me to do the job."

"She has been abducted."

"Do we know who by?"

The brigadier gave a kind of wince. "Yes and no. Jeff received a video which I'll show you later. The man who sent it calls himself Hussein-i Sabbah."

"Wasn't that the name of the Persian head of the Hashishim?"

"Hassan-i Sabbah, founder of the Nizari Ismai'li sect, otherwise known as the Hashishim. Precisely. And you are quite right; Hussein is the diminutive of Hassan. The thing is, we have no record of this man. Neither have Central Intelligence or the Federal Bureau of Investigation. I have spoken to ODIN—"

"Odin? The Norse god?" I smiled. "I didn't realize you were so well connected, sir."

He narrowed his eyes, and his mouth twitched like he wasn't sure whether to laugh or not. "They are unofficial, like us. They don't really exist, but they manage and coordinate the flow of intelligence from the Five Eyes."

"I thought the NSA did that."

"They wish. However, the point is ODIN hasn't heard of him either."

"So he's a rogue operator."

"That was the initial view, but there are indications he may have wider and deeper connections. He makes reference to things that only a well-connected operator would have knowledge of."

"Like?"

"Training camps and bases in Iran, events in East Africa no one would know about unless they were well connected. I'll acquaint you with all of this in a moment. But first let me make this clear: Cobra cannot employ you to find this girl. That is not our brief. We are exclusively concerned with eliminating a particular class of international criminal, as you know. On the other hand, we don't have the kind of information that would allow us to classify this Hussein-i Sabbah as one of that class of criminal—as having committed crimes against humanity, and thus have a justified reason to send you after him."

I frowned. "So what am I doing here?"

He smiled. "You are not here. You are up in the Wind River Mountains. What I have suggested to Jeff is that he employ you, privately, to recover his daughter—"

I interrupted him. "Sir, I am a soldier, not a detective. That is a job for the feds. They have the skills and the resources."

He shook his head. "In the first place, between us, Cobra and the Clearwater Corporation have technological resources that the FBI can only dream about. In the second place, working directly for Jeff, you have unlimited access to a hundred billion dollars in financial resources. In addition to that, he cannot *brief* the Bureau. He cannot give them a task— a mission—and tell them how he wants it done. If he reported it to the Bureau, their protocols would kick in, and the machine would take over. As a result, they would investigate, Beverly would get killed, or worse, and Hussein would disappear. But if he briefs *you*, secretly, with no press coverage or leaky officials involved, they will not be expecting you. And you will have a very precise brief, a brief the FBI could never have: Bring Beverly safely home and kill Hussein-i Sabbah."

TWO

He reached down to the table by his side and pressed a remote control. The lights dimmed, and a TV screen emerged from the cabinet against the wall. It remained black for a moment. Then suddenly there was a young girl. She was about fourteen or fifteen but still childlike. Her face showed she was terrified, her cheeks glistened with tears, her eyes were puffy and red, and her mouth was pulled down in an expression of grief and fear. I felt a hot coal of rage in my belly.

A man appeared from off-screen and sat next to her. He was in a white robe and had a white turban wound around his head, but his face was obscured by a black scarf. Behind them, there was a window, but it had been smeared over with black paint, and only a couple of glimmers of light shone through at the edges. There were faint, dim noises which were hard to distinguish. The girl's sobbing was clearly audible. The man spoke suddenly. His voice was slightly muffled by the scarf.

"Good morning, Mr. Cook. How does it feel to be the richest man in the world today?" He had a very slight accent, but his English was that of a man who had been through an elite English education—Eton or Harrow and then Oxford. "How does the value of all that wealth stack up against the loss of your daughter? Do you feel rich and privileged right now?"

He stopped talking and looked down at the floor.

"I'll tell you what I think, Mr. Cook. I think that right now"—he raised his head to look at the camera again—"you are the poorest man on the planet. Because you have lost the only truly valuable thing you had, and your world is now a world of pain." He shook his head. "It does not get any better. It only gets worse and more painful. I will tell you what comes next. I will marry your daughter, and she will become my possession, my chattel. We will live together in Sartakht. I will beat her often to keep her in submission. She will bear me children, and she will raise them to be great warriors and heroes. You will see them born, and you will see their birthdays. You will see them graduate to Rafsanjan, and you will see your daughter raise them, like the cow, like the breeding beast that she is. And one day, Mr. Cook, your daughter will be raped by my men. I will accuse her of adultery, and she will be executed, buried up to her neck in sand, and stoned to death. I will film the whole thing for you so that you can have a record of your daughter's useful life and death."

He spread his hands. "Can you stop this from happening? Of course. Obedience and subjugation will always bring God's favor. But I do not have to tell you exactly what to do. Your own conscience will guide you. We will talk, Mr. Cook. You can crawl to me on your knees, and you can tell me what steps you have taken to bring God's favor upon you."

He turned to Beverly. "You want to say some words to your father?"

She nodded and spoke through her sobs. "I love you, Daddy, and tell Aunt Bella Aurora I love her and miss her. And please, follow the path of subjugation to God."

Hussein leaned forward toward the camera, and it went black. The lights came up. I said, "Who is Aunt Bella Aurora?"

"We have no idea, and Jeff has no idea either. We are trying to work it out."

"What about the noises and the patches of light through the pane on the window?"

"We have forensic specialists working on both, but so far, we have very little to go on."

I nodded. Something was nagging at the back of my mind. While I let the back of my mind work at it, I said, "Sartakht and Rafsanjan, what are these places?"

He gave a single nod and took a pull on his drink. As he set it down, he said, "It's what I mentioned to you earlier. There are very few people that know about either of those places. The fact that he knows about both says a lot. Sartakht is a training camp deep in the Zagros mountain range. It specializes in very particular kinds of terrorism, from cyber terrorism to mental conditioning and esoteric stuff like that. Rafsanjan is a research center, part of a network that specializes in weapons of mass destruction. Both have close ties with a number of terrorist organizations. Not just jihadist ones, either. They are working increasingly closely with Russia and North Korea."

"So where do I start?"

"You'll do it?"

"Of course. But I'm not real clear yet what *it* is. How did the abduction happen? Were there any witnesses? Do we have any forensics, fingerprints, DNA...?" He drew breath to answer, but I interrupted him. "Why is Cook not here to tell me himself?"

He shook his head. "There can be no personal contact between you and Cook. He must have absolute deniability, not just plausible but indisputable. Besides, I can take you through the whole thing, probably better than he can."

"You were there?" I tried to keep the irony out of my voice but didn't do a great job.

"No, and neither was he. But where he is emotionally distraught, I am not. So I can be more objective. Shall I walk you through what we know?"

"Yeah."

He pulled an old-fashioned rope hanging from the ceiling beside his chair, and a moment later, a man in a white jacket with white gloves stepped in. The brigadier said, "We'll need some sandwiches—cheese, ham, pickles, you know the sort of thing."

The man muttered that he knew and withdrew. The brigadier sipped his whisky, and as he set down his glass, he said, "I mentioned that Beverly was home schooled. She had a number of tutors for specific subjects, but then there was one tutor who gave her a solid grounding in general knowledge—a basic educational foundation, as it were."

"His name?"

"Oliver Brown. He appeared to have good references, which were followed up—"

"How long ago was that?"

"Two years ago last July, shortly after Adriana's death."

"Adriana was the mother?"

"Yes. Oliver spent August preparing the curriculum, and they started their lessons toward the end of September. They were apparently fond of him. He was by all accounts a good teacher. Beverly liked him, and he never showed any signs of eccentricity, religious fanaticism, or anything peculiar of that nature."

There was a knock at the door, and a pretty maid in uniform came in and placed two plates of sandwiches on a table between us. She gave me a smile and withdrew. I picked up a ham sandwich and said, "From the way you're talking, you think he took the girl."

He kind of winced. "The fact is voice recognition software has him as *probably* the man on the video. In terms of build, he is roughly the same. Oliver had a normal West Coast accent. The man in the video has more of a Middle Eastern accent, but an accent is the easiest thing in the world to imitate."

I was frowning as I chewed. I watched him reach for a cheese sandwich. "Sir, voice recognition is pretty compelling evidence. Add to that the fact that he was familiar with the family's movements and with Beverly's timetable, and it's a pretty strong case. Yet I can see you have doubts."

"You're absolutely right." He said it around a chunk of sandwich he was chewing. "Everything points to him. My only reservation is that I know Oliver, and I am a pretty good judge of men, and I just don't see Oliver doing something like this. It takes a lot of grit to plan and, above all, execute an operation of this sort. Oliver just didn't strike me as the type." He raised his shoulders an eighth of an inch. "But again, all that means is that I may not be as sharp as I believe I am. Or that Oliver, like many sociopaths, is an extremely good liar."

I grunted and sipped my whiskey. "So what happened?"

He picked up his glass and sat back. "Four days ago—" He paused to look at his watch. "Yes, almost exactly four days ago,

Jeff took his car and drove down to San Jose. That's where Clearwater has its head office. It was what he did every Monday, Wednesday, and Friday. The rest of the time he worked from home. When he was at the office, he left his daughter in the care of her tutor—"

"Oliver Brown."

"Correct—Angelita, the nanny, and Mrs. Noaks, the cook. Part of the day, there was also a cleaner. She came in from nine until four, then went home. Jeff would have left the office at four, and by then, Beverly would have been in the care of Mrs. Noaks."

"What time did Cook come home?"

"It's a three-hour drive from San Jose. He left the office at four to beat the rush hour and arrived home at just after seven."

"By which time, Beverly would have been alone with her nanny and the cook for two and a half hours."

The brigadier nodded. "Yes, only she wasn't there. The front door was open, Angelita's car was there, but there was no sign of Angelita, Mrs. Noaks, or Beverly. Jeff called to them but got no response—until he went into the kitchen."

There was a horrible inevitability about it. I said, "He found them there dead."

"They had both, Angelita and Mrs. Noaks, been shot in the head. A single shot. Mrs. Noaks in the left temple, where she was sitting at the kitchen table, and Angelita between the eyes, as though she had turned from what she was doing at the sink."

"So he is unemotional and well-trained. Probably a professional."

"It certainly looks that way."

"Does that sound like the tutor, Oliver Brown?"

"No, not in the least."

"And Cook's first reaction was to call you?"

"It was clear Beverly had been abducted, and he knew that I could get her back more quickly and more efficiently than a state bureaucracy."

I frowned. "How come he knows about Cobra?"

"He doesn't, though as a major defense contractor, he has top security clearance. Besides which, he knows that I am involved in black ops for the US and the UK. So we got a couple teams in to go over the house, and we got exactly nothing. There were the fingerprints you would expect to get, and aside from that, only negatives. The house had not been broken into, there were no boot prints, powder burns, stray hairs, bits of cotton—nothing. A minor consolation was that there were no traces of blood either, other than those from Mrs. Noaks and Angelita."

"So we can say that the abduction took place some time between four p.m. when the cleaner left and seven when Cook got home."

"Yes, that's how I see it."

"What about the cleaner?"

"A retired village woman, three generations in the town, absolutely no connections with crime or terrorism. We have screened her and questioned her. She's in the clear."

"What about the cops?"

"They have been instructed to stand down, it's being taken care of at a higher level."

"So the only person unaccounted for is Oliver Brown, the tutor, and voice recognition places him as the guy in the video."

The brigadier nodded. "Not one hundred percent, but very probably."

"What do you know about his background?"

"Native of Napa, sixty miles down the hill, younger brother, older sister, middle-class family, comfortably well off, did well at school, Methodist but not practicing, degree from UCLA in psychology, trained as a teacher. No record of any kind. Generally unremarkable."

"Obviously you've checked his online presence."

"Facebook, X, Reddit, LinkedIn, and we checked his messaging services and telephone records. Either he was working solo or, as is increasingly the case these days, he was using conventional craft, dead drops, physical meetings face to face, coded classified ads..."

"Cold war stuff."

"Effective and very hard to trace."

I pointed at the black TV screen. "I want to watch that again a few times tonight. Can you make it available in my room?"

"Of course."

"And send it to my phone."

"Sure. I'll send you a photograph of Oliver too."

"And I want to go and see Oliver's parents and Cook's house."

"That's arranged already. We fly in..." He looked at his watch. "Six hours."

I made to stand. "I'm going to get some sleep. Am I in the same room?"

"Your room, yes."

"Is there anything else I need to know?"

He gave his head a single shake. "You have the basics. You understand, whoever did this, we don't want them alive."

"I know." I stood and hesitated. "Is there any chance Oliver was taken too?"

He smiled. "I know. It's the first thing that comes to mind. But it seems to be him in that video. The simplest explanation, Harry, is that we are looking at a dissociative personality disorder."

"A split personality?"

He mixed a shrug with a nod. "It's more like two distinct personalities inhabiting one mind. But right now, the evidence points to the fact that Oliver Brown has abducted Beverly Cook. And if that is the case, then we hunt him down, and we kill him."

I nodded, left him sitting by the fire, and made my way up the old mahogany stairs to my room. There I sat on the end of the bed and played the video over several times until all I could hear in my head was the fear in Beverly's voice as she sobbed out, "I love you, Daddy, and tell Aunt Bella Aurora I love her and miss her. And please, follow the path of subjugation to God."

"...tell Aunt Bella Aurora I love her..."

I went and showered, hot then cold, then hot and cold again and came back to the bed drying my hair. I put the video on again, over and over, and the more I listened to it, the more I filtered out his voice and her voice and focused on the sounds, faint and distant, that came through the painted glass. As I did so, it became more and more obvious that if they had painted the glass, it was because whatever was out there was recognizable. And if that was true, whatever sounds were out there would be recognizable too.

"...Bella Aurora..."

Her voice echoed in my mind. Her voice, sobbing in the desert, staring at me, pleading at me with her huge, dark eyes as Mohammed Ben-Amini, the Butcher of Al-Landy, murdered and raped her village, and she cried out, *"...tell Aunt Bella Aurora I love her..."* while the great steam pistons thudded and groaned in the background and I sank into an agony of darkness.

I sat up with a fierce jolt in my heart and reached for the phone.

"Harry? Is everything OK?"

"Yeah. Sorry to wake you, sir. I need the tech guys to isolate those background noises."

"They are barely audible."

"I don't care. Get them to do the best they can. As soon as possible."

"I'll tell them. Get some sleep. We fly in three hours."

I hung up, fell back, and sank into deep sleep.

THREE

We touched down at Hoberg Airfield at Seigler Springs at ten a.m. that morning. I wasn't sure as I climbed down from the plane into the middle of a field whether we were somewhere in the middle of nowhere, or nowhere in the middle of somewhere. You could see it was California because the sky was that special California blue. There were scattered oaks and pines and dusty hills and not much else besides a Range Rover and a Mercedes with smoked windows. The Mercedes pulled away as we approached the Range Rover, and nobody said a word.

From the airfield, it was a fifteen-minute drive, first along the Seigler Canyon Road as far as Route 29 and then Point Lakeview Road through a landscape of flat, well-tended fields as far as Thurston Lake. After that, it was a winding path through dense woodland all the way to the small, exclusive town of Clearlake Riviera.

Cook's house was on the shores of the lake, overlooking the dark water. The first impression as we approached from the village was of a small fortress out of a sci-fi movie. A sheer wall of some fourteen feet in height projected from the building, creating a large forecourt at the front, which was accessed through a large, steel electronic gate. It was twenty feet across and probably thirty feet long with another steel gate which I figured was the parking garage at the far end. Before that was a large, glass door which at first glance you'd have thought was a mirror. That was where the brigadier stopped the Range Rover as the steel gate closed behind us. He pointed at the oblong glare of the glass and opened his door.

"One-way bulletproof glass reinforced with carbon nanotubes. It's harder than steel. From the inside, you can see whoever is at the door from head to foot in perfect detail. All they can see is themselves—their own reflection."

We climbed out, and he approached the door, pressing a green button on a fob he pulled from his pocket. From an invisible panel in the door, I saw a laser scan him, and a gender-less voice said, "Good morning, Brigadier. Please say a few words."

"Good morning, Chris. It's a beautiful day."

"It is a beautiful day here in California. Please come in and make yourself at home." The door slid open, and as we stepped over the threshold, the voice said, "If there is anything you need, please don't hesitate to tell me."

The door closed behind us, and I wondered what we would have to do to leave if we were in a hurry. The brigadier glanced at me, probably reading my thoughts on my face.

"Welcome to twenty-first century California."

"A key and a steel bolt are faster, more reliable, and less vulnerable to hacking and EMPs."

"I agree. They are also less likely to decide you are an impractical waste of resources. Come, let me show you."

It was the kind of house where rooms would have been considered primitive and perhaps a little amusing. This was the sort of house where instead of rooms you had spaces. The floors were all dark wood with a high polish, and low bookcases and furniture replaced walls. From where we stood at the entrance space, we could see a broad dining area to the left. The table was a thick, oval slab of glass standing on a huge chunk of irregularly shaped, highly polished green granite. Beyond it, there was an ancient, battered Castilian dresser with a large stone vase holding a spray of sunflowers. Directly ahead, two broad steps took you down to the relaxing-sitting area, where huge calico sofas were strewn with carefully designed disregard among overstuffed armchairs and chesterfields. On the floors, there were sheepskin rugs and built into the wall, a fireplace with a copper hood.

The wall there was glass, and a sliding door gave on to a lawn and a large pool. At the end of the lawn, maybe sixty or seventy yards away, there was another wall and beyond that the lake.

I pointed. "Is that a possible point of entry?"

He shook his head. "He recognized that as a weak spot, and it is bristling with electronic surveillance and alarms that connect in real time to the house, his office, and private security down the road. None of that was triggered."

We crossed the space and stepped down to what would have been the living room. Beyond it was a white, rustic, Mediterranean arch, and through it, there was a kitchen the size of a New York apartment. It contained a vast steel fridge, a pine table with comfortable space for six people, and all the usual kitchen gadgets with a few that would have looked more at home in a laboratory. The only thing that was out of place was the large, dry bloodstain at the far end of the table. The brigadier pointed to it.

"Mrs. Noaks was sitting there peeling potatoes. She still had the small kitchen knife in her right hand and a half-peeled potato in her left." He pointed beyond her chair to the sink at the far wall. There was dry blood around the sink and on the floor and spatter on the wall. "It looks as though Angelita was making coffee. She must have turned when she heard the noise. The coffee pot was on the surface, ready to go on the stove. She was slumped on the floor with a hole through her head. Both slugs were 9mm from the same weapon."

I sighed heavily. There was a small video monitor by the stove with a telephone attached. I pointed at it. "Anyone trying to get in would be seen there, I'm guessing."

He nodded. "It's an isolated system. You can't hack into it. You either have access through a fob or you have to be let in from inside."

"This place is a high-tech fortress. Whoever killed them and took Beverly had already been admitted and was trusted. He was standing right next to the cook, and she never saw it coming. And Angelita—" I pointed over at the sink. "She had her back to him, making coffee. They must have known he was in the kitchen. Mrs. Noaks would have seen him come in."

He gave a small shrug. "Everything points to Oliver." He seemed to think for a moment, but the small wince he made suggested it was something he had thought through and rejected several times already. "The only option is that it was someone known either to Oliver or Mrs. Noaks and Angelita, and he took Oliver as a hostage along with Beverly."

I shook my head. "With all due respect, sir, you don't believe that, and neither do I. Beverly is a high-value target. Nobody gives a damn about Oliver. It's hard to see how this played out without Oliver being at the very least involved as a participant." We were both quiet for a moment, me scanning the kitchen and him watching me. I said, "It is weird that he has no previous visible criminal or terrorist connections, but it's like the old Sherlock Holmes dictum. Eliminate the impossible, and whatever is left, however improbable, is the truth. The fact that it's weird doesn't make it impossible."

"Agreed. As I suggested to you last night, we may be dealing with a very sophisticated, low-tech cell operating along Cold War lines. Or if we are lucky, he may just be a lone operator suffering from some kind of dissociative personality disorder."

I grunted. "Let's just hope Mr. Hyde hasn't got an IQ of one-seventy."

We went over the house, more for me to satisfy myself that I had observed due diligence than in the hopes of finding anything. The brigadier's boys and Cook's best men had already gone over the place with fine-toothed combs. So far, they had turned up nothing, and I wasn't real optimistic that I was about to.

In Beverly's room, there were digital picture frames on the walls, fluffy dogs and bears on her bed, and a giant TV screen on the wall. But that room, like the house, was empty of any useful data. Out of the window, I stared at the black water of the lake. The brigadier was standing in the doorway, watching me. I shook my head.

"There is nothing here," I said. "Let's go talk to Oliver's parents."

We took Route 29 down to Napa and then turned west to Sonoma. We took it easy, and it was about a two-hour drive along rough, country roads among woodlands and rolling hills that felt strangely remote from the technological, urban heartlands of San Francisco and Los Angeles.

Sonoma itself, settled among broad vineyards at the foot of the Mission Highlands, felt strangely rural and bucolic, though we were just twenty miles from the urban sprawl of the Bay Area.

The Browns had their house on Donald Street, set back from the road in the shade of a small sequoia which dominated an overgrown front yard. The brigadier had called to let them know we were coming, and as I stood looking at the yard, the door opened, and a rotund woman with very red cheeks stood watching us with eyes that said she was about ready for some good news. She said, "Are you...?"

The brigadier gave her a smile that was as reassuring as it was dishonest.

"Mrs. Brown? I am Brigadier Alexander Byrd, and this is my associate Mr. Harry Bauer. Is this a good time?"

"Yes, of course. We're a bit worried. My husband's in the living room..."

She said it like that was the reason she was worried. She moved back to let us into a small entrance hall where there were boots and hats and coats and a door with glass panels that stood open onto a living room where a man in an old gray cardigan stood watching us and frowning.

"Are you police officers?" he said. "It's been days now, and we've heard nothing from the police."

"George—" It was Mrs. Brown behind us. "Don't antagonize them. He always antagonizes people..."

The brigadier stepped toward the man with his hand outstretched. "We are investigators, Mr. Brown, but we are not police. I am Brigadier Alexander Byrd, and this is Sergeant Harry Bauer."

George Brown shook the brigadier's hand, though his frown had deepened into uncertainty.

"The Army? What has the Army got to do with my son?"

"Nothing, Mr. Brown. May we sit down?"

Mr. Brown pointed to a couple of chairs and lowered himself, still frowning, back into the chair he had just risen from. Mrs. Brown sat on the sofa with her hands clasped in her lap.

"Before we go any further"—the brigadier looked at each of them in turn—"I need to tell you that this is a matter of national security, and I need to be sure that you will discuss this with nobody."

Mr. Brown's frown descended into a scowl. "I think I am about ready to see some ID." The brigadier pulled a wallet from his inside pocket and handed it over. Brown stared at it a moment, then stared at the brigadier. "Pentagon? You want to tell me what my son has to do with the Pentagon?"

"Once again," said the brigadier, taking back his wallet with his fake ID, "I need your assurance that you understand this is a matter of national security, and you will discuss it with nobody."

Brown nodded. "Understood." His wife nodded too.

"You are aware that your son was tutoring Jeff Cook's daughter. I am not sure if you are aware of it, but Jeff Cook is the founder and CEO of the Clearwater Corporation, which is a major defense contractor."

Brown's face was a study in sudden and terrible realization.

He grew gray by degrees, and when he spoke, his voice was barely a whisper. "What has happened...?"

"Beverly, his student, Jeff Cook's daughter, has gone missing, two members of the household staff have been murdered, and Oliver has also gone missing."

Mrs. Brown gave a small scream and covered her mouth with both hands. Her eyes were screwed tight. Mr. Brown gripped the arm of his chair like he had lost his balance despite being seated. He said, "Oh God..." and eased himself back. "Oh dear God, this can't be true."

The brigadier gave them a moment, then began to speak. "I must apologize for being slow in contacting you, but I am sure you will realize, when you give it a moment's thought, that this is a situation with major national security implications."

It was Mrs. Brown who answered. Her voice was shrill, bordering on hysterical. "You can't think—Oliver is not, he would never, he's barely a kid..."

The brigadier was shaking his head. "Your son is not under suspicion, Mrs. Brown. The Clearwater Corporation screened him thoroughly when he was first employed, and we have since done a deep background check. We are quite certain your son was not involved in the abduction, and this is partly what worries us. Because—I am assuming you have not heard from him or the kidnappers, which leaves us only two options. Either he has been kidnapped along with Beverly, or he has rescued her, and they have fled together."

Hope, pathetic and shallow, touched their faces. She said, "But he would have contacted us!"

"Not if he feared it would bring danger to you. He may be hoping that you, or the investigators charged with the case, with your help, might deduce where he would go into hiding."

He paused, looking from one to the other as they stared at each other, seeking inspiration in each other as to where their son might be.

After a moment, the brigadier went on. "Is there any place —think hard, is there any place that he might go to, resort to, in a moment of panic? A place that is meaningful to him, a place nobody else would think of, a cabin you used to vacation in, a beach house, an apartment where you used to live..."

She said, "My sister's house..."

He snapped, "Don't be ridiculous!"

The brigadier leaned toward Mrs. Brown. "Tell me, what about your sister's house?"

"It was when he was just seven or eight years old. We went through a hard patch financially, and my sister Beth took us in. He loved her. They had a kind of special connection." She glanced at her husband. He sighed noisily and looked away. She went on. "She died a couple of years ago and left her house to Oliver. He's never done anything with it because it's way over on the East Coast, in Connecticut. But I suppose if he wanted somewhere safe, and not implicate us, he might have gone there."

"Can you give us the address, Mrs. Brown?"

She rose and went in search of pen and paper. I looked at her husband. His eyes were bloodshot, and he was beginning to look like he had a bad cold, fighting back the tears. I said, "If he hadn't gone there, Mr. Brown, can you think of anywhere else he might have gone?"

He shook his head. "Home," he said. "He should have come home..."

Five minutes later, we left them to their grief and horror and made our way back to the Range Rover. I climbed in the passenger seat as the brigadier got behind the wheel. He slammed the door, and I said, "It's a long shot. If he's abducted her, he won't go to that house. And that room with the painted window"—I shook my head—"it doesn't exactly scream Connecticut."

"No." He nodded. "I agree, but unless we get something from the lab, it's the only shot we've got."

FOUR

WE PARTED AT THE AIRPORT AFTER LUNCH AND A long conversation. He took a scheduled flight back to New York, and I took the company plane to New Haven, Connecticut. It was a five-hour flight, and by the time I'd boarded the Gulfstream, it was already five in the afternoon with an ETA of just after ten p.m.

Over a martini with more dry than martini, I stretched my legs and played the video again with Beverly telling her dad to follow the path of subjugation to God. That part was what she had been told to say. That much was obvious. But her request —her plea—that he should tell Aunt Bella Aurora that she loved her and missed her, that was a message. The more I thought about it, the more I heard her repeat it, the more convinced I was that she was sending her father a message. Aunt Bella didn't exist.

They brought me a steak and fries and a bottle of Antica Terra, and as I ate, I stared out, unseeing, at our vast continent as it slipped slowly by beneath me. Aunt Bella didn't exist. I couldn't see what that meant, but I knew in my bones—in the marrow of my bones—I knew the answer was in those words.

After the meal, I connected my phone to the monitor beside my table and watched the video again. I tried to ignore her voice and focus on the painted window and the background noises. The cracks of light told me nothing, but phasing out her voice and trying to focus my mind on the other, dim sounds that came through, I thought I could catch the unmistakable sound of diesel engines, maybe heavy machinery.

That made sense up to a point. If I had abducted a young girl and wanted to hold her while I demanded a ransom, I might well take her to a disused warehouse or building in an industrial park.

I watched it a couple more times—maybe six or seven—and with her words going around in my head, pulling me into darkness, I found myself waking suddenly as we hit the tarmac at New Haven, on the east shore of the bay. I had, at San Francisco Airport, booked a room at the Omni in town, and I had a Mustang waiting for me at the car rentals. And by the time I picked up my car, I was beat and seriously tempted to crash at the hotel and check out Oliver Brown's house in the morning. In any case, I was pretty sure of what I was going to find there, and that was a whole lot of nothing. But the outside chance that Beverly might be there, tied, gagged, and terrified made me turn right onto the turnpike and head east toward Branford and Stony Creek, where the house stood on Leetes Island Road.

It was just over ten miles from the airport. Most of the way was on I-95, among scattered villages and abundant woodland that looked dark and massive in the limpid glow of the turnpike lamps.

At Branford, I came off onto Leetes Island Road and was immediately enveloped by darkness and dense trees. I followed the amber glow of my headlights past occasional cottages set back from the road among well-tended lawns and areas where the woodlands were so dense they seemed to form tunnels through the blackness.

Pretty soon I could smell the salt tang of ozone through the open windows, and I came to an intersection at the heart of what looked like a small village of clapboard houses with gabled roofs and tall chimneys. There were no streetlamps here, but a few porch lights were on, and a warm glow seeped here and there between heavy drapes.

I turned left and followed the road along for three or four hundred yards till I came to a driveway half concealed among dense trees and bushes. The name and number on the mailbox told me this was the place. So I pulled in behind some bushes, out of sight of the road, and killed the engine.

I sat for a while, watching the dark windows, waiting for a drape to move or a face to appear, peering out at me. Nothing happened. After ten minutes, I climbed out of the Mustang and crossed the dirt drive to the porch. I could hear no sounds through the door, and no light filtered out through the drapes. I crossed the lawn, which was dense and overgrown, to the back of the house.

There the kitchen window had no drapes, and all I could see through the glass was a dark, empty room with a round pine table at which there was no sign of anybody having eaten.

Beyond that I could make out a hallway but no glow of any light. No sign of life or habitation.

I was telling myself Oliver Brown's house had been nothing but a red herring and a serious waste of time right from the start, when my eye fell again on the back door—the kitchen door.

It's a completely unscientific theory of mine, founded on nothing but my own, subjective experience, that people will put secure—even high-tech—locks and alarms on their front doors and the glass doors onto their back yards while leaving simple Mortice locks on their kitchen doors. I approached and had a look.

Clearly, whatever Oliver Brown might have become as he grew to manhood, his aunt had not expected a home invasion or a burglary, much less to house the abducted daughter of a billionaire defense contractor. The lock was an old-fashioned sash Mortice. I had seen no sign of an alarm, and logic suggested that if Oliver had not taken possession of the house, the basic utilities and any alarm systems would be disconnected.

I took the Swiss Army knife from my pocket, selected the screwdriver, fitted it to the lock, and gave it a firm thump with the heel of my hand, then turned. The door opened easily. No lights flashed, no alarms screamed. God bless Connecticut.

I stepped over the threshold and closed the door behind me. Then I hunkered down, closed my eyes, and counted slowly to sixty. When I opened them, the dim light from the kitchen window was enough for me to make out the kitchen table and chairs, the refrigerator, the dishwasher, and the washing machine under the work surface. I stood and examined the sink and the small drying rack next to it. They were both dry. The dishwasher was empty and also dry. Nobody had used either in a while.

The fridge told a similar story. It was switched off and empty. I looked for a door to a basement. There wasn't one.

I walked through to the small hallway where pale light filtered through two glass panels in the front door. There was a door on the right which I figured led to the living room and a staircase on the left that rose to the bedrooms.

In the living room, there was what you'd expect: a sofa, two armchairs, a TV, and a dresser with a few photographs. Beyond it was a small dining table with four chairs set beside the glass doors that led to the back yard. There was no sign of Oliver or Beverly. There was no sign they had ever been there.

I mounted the stairs out of a sense of due diligence. I had to be able to state categorically that the place was empty and uninhabited and had been that way for a long time. The three bedrooms upstairs confirmed that. The beds were unmade, the mattresses wrapped in plastic, the closets empty. In the bathroom, everything had been cleaned, and there were zero toiletries. The trip to Connecticut had been a total waste of time. A hot ember of anger smoldered in my belly. Hours of precious time had been thrown away, hours in which Beverly might have suffered unspeakable horrors.

Her words came to me again. *Tell Aunt Bella I love her.*

Aunt Bella. Not Aunt Beth.

I descended the stairs, and it was then, as I made for the kitchen, with my eyes now fully adjusted to the darkness, that I saw the door under the stairs. It was made of the same wood as the staircase and was almost invisible in the dark. There was a small brass lock but no handle. What made me frown was that on closer inspection, I found the key in the lock. I pulled my Sig from behind my back, held the key at its edges, turned, and pushed. The door creaked softly as it opened, but what really drew my attention was the dim light that filtered up from the bottom of the stairs.

The light was steady. It was not the light of a flame. It was either battery generated or electric. I waited and listened with my weapon trained on the foot of the stairs. I heard nothing. Nothing moved. I repressed a wild hope that I was going to find Beverly down there. In my mind, I could see her, bound and gagged on a chair, and my belly burned.

I stepped onto the small landing. From there, I could see a concrete floor and the end of the wooden banisters. The light was too bright to be from a flashlight or a battery-powered lamp. Which meant that contrary to what I had assumed, the power to the house had been reconnected. I needed to know who by.

The stairs were concrete, and I descended four of them quickly and in silence. All I could see was more of the concrete floor, but my next step would make my feet visible to anybody who was down there. I waited, listening, but could still hear nothing.

I crouched down and jumped the remaining seven steps, turning as I went. I landed in a squat with the Sig held out in front of me, trained on the guy sitting in the armchair beside the furnace.

At first, he seemed quite placid. But as I stood, I noticed that his fingertips had torn deep into the arms of the old chair and his forehead was badly bruised, showing clearly the mark of the four fingers of a left hand that must have held the head motionless against violent pressure. The head itself was sitting in the man's lap.

The blood had sprayed in a wide arc across the floor, more abundant on his left, then diminishing toward the right, suggesting that his killer had come at him from behind, pulled his head back with his left hand, then cut from left to right with a razor-sharp knife. By the time he had reached the right ear, Oliver Brown had already bled out and was dead.

The front of his shirt was caked, and the blood was largely dry. Time of death is practically impossible to tell from the condition of a body or the dryness of the blood, but what was clear was that he had not been killed in the last hour or two. He had been here long enough for the blood to start to dry.

I took a few photographs and climbed the stairs back to the hall, closed the door, and pulled my cell from my pocket. The brigadier answered on the first ring.

"Harry."

"I found Oliver."

The tone of my voice must have told him I hadn't found him sitting watching TV or spoon-feeding Beverly. He said, "Oh, where?"

"In the basement of his Aunt Beth's house. He's been decapitated. I'm sending you pictures of the scene. You need to get a forensic team down here. I am leaving the scene exactly as I found it, except that I picked the lock in the back door to the kitchen."

"Good. I'll arrange it."

"I want to get out of here pretty fast. I'll call you from the car. But before I do, points to note while they are fresh in my mind: He was sitting comfortably in an old armchair in the basement. The electricity was connected in the house. The only immediate sign of violence was the bruising on his fore-head. That was the mark of a left hand holding his head back while his throat was cut. Finally, the killer left the light on in the basement and the key in the basement door under the stairs."

I sent him the photographs I had taken and made my way back out through the kitchen door to my car.

FIVE

I WAS IN THE TUNNEL OF DARK TREES AGAIN, chasing the glow of my headlamps fast along Leetes Island Road toward the Turnpike. I called the brigadier again and asked him, "Where are you, sir?"

"At my apartment on Riverside Drive. You're about an hour and a half from Manhattan."

"I figure that. Do we have anything from the lab yet about the video?"

"Some initial results. Tell me your thoughts on what you found first. Then we'll discuss the lab's findings."

"Oliver knew his killer. He was sitting on that old chair in the basement, and his killer came up behind him, grabbed his forehead with his left hand, and cut his throat from left to right before beheading him. Oliver didn't react or struggle until his killer already had a grip on his head."

"Agreed."

"Second, Oliver was killed by the same person who killed Mrs. Noaks and Angelita."

"Based on what?"

"It's that same basic technique, the same MO if you like. Gain their confidence, get them comfortable with you, then take them unawares with clinical precision. This killer feels nothing when killing. The only way we could attribute these murders to Oliver was by assuming a split personality. That assumption didn't sit well with you, sir, because you had never seen any indication of it before. Now we don't need that assumption. Oliver's own murder fits the pattern of the previous murders."

"All right. Good point."

I slowed and turned onto I-95, headed west toward New Haven, and began to accelerate.

"A final point, sir: I think Oliver was being blackmailed or coerced in some way. The way it looks is Oliver was befriended by his killer and gained access to the Cooks' household through him and befriended Mrs. Noaks and Angelita, and above all Beverly, but always while Jeff was away at work. Why nobody ever mentioned this guy to Cook I don't know, but I can guess. Someone security conscious enough to build that fortress is not going to welcome some unknown guy visiting on a regular basis while he is not at home. So it was probably a tacit—or explicit—understanding that there was no need to mention it."

"That is probably correct, Harry. Jeff would not have been happy about that, and they must all have known it."

"And by the looks of it, he was right to feel that way. From what you've told me about Oliver, it's unlikely he would have risked his job and Jeff's anger by willingly inviting this guy to the house. There is also the fact that, though his Aunt Beth's house was empty and showed no signs of being lived in, the electricity was connected. The killer must have persuaded him to do that for some reason. So I am figuring he was either blackmailing Oliver or coercing him somehow."

"That seems likely, yes."

"You mentioned an agency that coordinates Five Eyes intelligence."

"Yes, I'll have a word with them and see if they can look into Oliver's background. If we can find a vulnerability, perhaps we can find out who might have exploited it."

"Right. We also need to know who Oliver's friends were. Who did he hang out with? Two gets you twenty that for the last two or three weeks, he was hanging with whoever killed him. They were pals."

"Agreed. I'll get a team on it. Anything else?"

I watched the dimly illuminated road with its sleeping houses speeding past in the night and shook my head.

"Nothing comes to mind right now, no. What about the lab?"

"Very little, I'm afraid. They closed in on the luminous strips in the black paint in the window, but it was impossible to distinguish anything. They had a little more success with the background noises. They managed to isolate what sound like diesel engines, perhaps a turbine and, believe it or not, a seagull."

I nodded. "Yeah, I thought it might be a port."

"It narrows it a bit, but on the East Coast of the United States, it doesn't narrow it much."

"Shit!" I thumped the steering wheel with my fist.

"Something?"

"I have been so stupid, sir."

"Explain."

"I have been focusing on Aunt Bella, wondering what it meant and if there was a connection with Aunt Beth—"

"Both with a B?"

I ignored him and went on. "But I couldn't find anything, and what she said made no sense. But of course 'aunt' was just to disguise the name! We knew that because Cook had told us there was no Aunt Bella. The name was Bella Aurora! For Christ's sake! How could I be so stupid? It's the name of a ship!"

"I'll find it."

He hung up, and I accelerated to a hundred and twenty miles per hour. If Highway Patrol wanted to stop me, let them catch me.

It was an hour later, maybe less, as I was crossing Van Courtland Park, that my cell rang.

"Harry. The Bella Aurora is docked at the Court Street docks in Brooklyn. It seems there are abandoned factories and warehouses in the area, as well as squats and abandoned residential buildings. How far away are you?"

"Twenty minutes. I'll try and make it ten."

I took the FDR to Brooklyn Bridge, and eighteen minutes later, I was cruising down Court Street toward the docks, watching the steady decline from leafy neighborhoods with pavement cafés to the grim industrial docklands beyond the I-278 overpass. At that time of night, the place was pretty much dead and empty of traffic. I passed Red Hook Park on my right, and pretty soon, I could see the water up ahead of me. On my left, I had a ruined warehouse with a yard full of rusty junk, and on my right, there was a redbrick structure with roller blinds and no windows. Beyond that, there was a yard secured by a gray brick wall and two dilapidated houses with their windows blacked out with paint. One of them had a broken door with boards nailed across it. No light came from inside either one. Parked outside was a dark Range Rover with smoked windows. I pulled up behind it and climbed out with my right hand behind my back, holding the butt of my P226.

As I approached, the driver's door opened. My hand tightened on the butt of my semi, but it was the familiar long, lanky form of the brigadier that slipped out and swung down. He pointed at the broken door.

"It's unlikely to be that one. We'll start with the other." As he spoke, he pulled a key from his jacket pocket. It looked like a regular Yale key, but it had a large, bulky head. He slipped it in the lock. I heard it buzz softly and click, and he opened the door. "A bit more reliable than the Swiss Army knife," he said quietly and stepped over the threshold. I moved ahead of him into a filthy hall littered with crumbling plaster, wooden boards, and a wide variety of garbage from large, black trash bags and old broken furniture to a gutted PC from the '90s and even a small red plastic tricycle with blue wheels.

I moved carefully to a doorway on the left. There were hinges but no door, and through it, I could see pale amber light. When I poked my head in, I could see that the light came from a collapsed roof, most of which was lying on the floor in the form of rubble and broken beams. This part of the building had just one floor and was uninhabitable. I looked at the brigadier and shook my head.

I noticed he had produced a Micro Uzi from under his jacket. At less than a foot in length with the stock folded, it is one of the most lethal firearms ever constructed. With a muzzle velocity of one thousand one hundred feet per second and a rate of fire of one thousand two hundred rounds per minute, it could empty its extended forty-round magazine in two seconds while tearing its target into minced meat.

I picked my way across the rubble in the hall and started to mount the steps, keeping one eye where I was treading and another on the narrow landing above me. The brigadier was behind me, the Uzi held out in front of him aimed at the upper floor. He had a flashlight in his hand and his back against the wall, sidestepping up the stairs like a crab in my footsteps.

The top floor was lacking the chaos of the ground floor. There was dust and fallen plaster but no rubble or junk. A door on my right stood open onto a filthy toilet. Ahead of me, another door stood open. The brigadier's flashlight picked out an old brass bed with bare springs and no mattress. The rest of the room was bare.

I moved on to the next room. It was closed. The brigadier took up his position at an angle to the door. I stood beside it, turned the handle, and shoved it open as I dropped to one knee and scanned the room with my Sig held out in front of me.

We were too late.

I stood, holstered my Sig, and flipped on the flashlight on my cell. The chair was there, with the tape and the ropes hanging from it. Beside it was the chair Hussein-i Sabbah had sat in to send his message. The windows were there, where they were in the video, painted black, and six or seven feet from the chairs was a tripod with a camera still attached.

The brigadier stepped out to the landing, pulling his cell from his jacket. I approached the camera. I heard the brigadier speaking as I turned it to look at the screen. There was a new video on it.

He was saying, "The Bella Aurora you found on the Court

Street docks, has it sailed?" He walked back into the room, staring at me while he listened. "It has? When did it sail, and what is its destination?"

I glanced at the time and date on the screen in front of me. It had been recorded that morning at seven a.m. The brigadier said, "Yesterday afternoon? Five p.m. Stand by."

He raised his chin at me in inquiry because I was shaking my head. I showed him the screen. He started talking into the phone again. "I need to know ships that departed this immediate area after seven in the morning. Absolute maximum priority. I need that information *now*. And get me a forensics team to Court Street."

He hung up. I said, "We don't know they left in a boat. They could have gone by car, train, coach, plane..."

"Play the video."

I pressed play. The setup was pretty much as it had been before, only there was no glare from the scratches in the window. Beverly looked drawn and exhausted. Hussein-i Sabbah sat beside her.

"You were so sure poor Oliver was your man. How unfairly you judged him. He was an innocent, and as he began to realize what was happening, he tried his hardest to protect his pupil. He was ineffectual, of course. The US has no warrior spirit left. You believe so passionately in negotiation." He laughed. "You are traders now, not conquerors anymore. And traders believe everyone is pragmatic. So everything can be achieved by dialogue, negotiation. The pen is mightier than the sword." He laughed again. "Askander did not write away the Gordian knot, Mr. Cook. He severed it with a sword. I will be in touch in a few days to let you know how your daughter is. She has a little message for you, Mr. Cook."

He removed the gag in her mouth, and she looked into the camera from a dark, infinitely sad place in her soul.

"Daddy, I beg of you to listen to Mr. Hussein's wise words. I don't want to lose you. Every day I remember sitting on your knee while you read me Danielle Clode. I know I have to die, but I want you to find the true god before I do. Allahu Akbar."

Hussein fit her gag again and looked into the camera. "Goodbye, Mr. Cook."

The screen went black. I was already on my phone searching for Danielle Clode.

"Danielle Clode," I said, "author of *In Search of the Woman Who Sailed the World*."

"It makes sense," he said. "He had an entire continent at his disposal, and he came to the New York docks. It could be a red herring, but we haven't enough data to take alternative action. We have to gamble that she is on one of the ships that sailed shortly after seven this morning."

I nodded. "Assuming she did, what action do we take?"

"We identify the ship and insert you."

I gave something that wanted to be a one-sided smile. "How?"

"We'll cross that bridge when we get to it."

His phone rang, and he put it on speaker.

"Sir, a number of ships departed Court Street quay during the day. I'm thinking the one that will interest you is the *Keshti Khoda*. It is owned by the Universal Shipping Corporation registered in Panama with a Russian major shareholder name of Peter Sokolov. It departed the dock this morning at nine a.m. carrying a mixed cargo to the Mediterranean."

I said, "What makes that our ship?"

"Who is that, sir? Can I answer?"

The brigadier nodded. "Yes, he's an operative. Go ahead."

"First off, Sokolov has been involved in several official Russian visits to Iran, as a trade consultant and a negotiator. He has a lot of interests in Iran and is known to facilitate breaches of embargos through his international trade network. The name of the ship is itself Persian. Given that the abductor has named himself after Persia's most famous assassin, I think this ship is a good candidate.

"Your other ships have sailed variously to Denmark, Argentina, the UK, and South Africa. Granted that the UK seems to be becoming a qua-Islamic state, sir, no offense intended, but nothing else about that ship raises any red flags."

"Point taken. Track it. We assume target is onboard."

"Yes, sir."

I was frowning at him. "Is that Cobra?"

He shook his head. "It's a team set up by me and Jeff. It doesn't exist, and I am not here."

"OK. The *Keshti Khoda* departed New York about thirteen hours ago. Assuming an average speed of between fifteen and seventeen knots for a cargo ship, that puts her about two hundred and forty miles out to sea right now. That's about two hundred and ten nautical miles. The plan is get me on board. The question is how do we do that?"

"Is the captain party to the abduction? We don't know. Are the crew party to the abduction? We don't know..."

I interrupted him. "If I had to make an assumption, I'd say yes he is, no they aren't."

"At fifteen to seventeen knots, nonstop, we're looking at a crossing time of seven to ten days. Allow for Atlantic weather and a stopover at the Azores, we are looking at a more typical crossing of maybe fifteen to eighteen days. So our choice is either to board the ship in force in international waters before they reach the Azores or to insert you secretly at some point along the way."

"Again, how?"

He eyed me for a moment. "Did I mention Jeff was a defense contractor and we had access to black technology?"

SIX

AND SO IT WAS THAT AT ONE A.M. THE NEXT morning, I found myself aboard a prototype Lockheed Martin JetStar Mk III that didn't really exist, hurtling at eight hundred miles per hour across New York State toward the North Atlantic.

The brigadier had driven us to Teterboro, where we had boarded an unmarked helicopter which had flown us, faster than any chopper I had ever been in before, one hundred and fifty miles to a small town called Owego. There we had spent a couple of hours at an underground facility that also didn't exist beneath a major facility that did exist as a major contractor to the DoD.

The guys there had provided us, without question, with the JetStar and various other items that they referred to as research projects which did not yet officially exist. I guess the billionaire club looks out for each other.

The *Keshti Khoda* was by then some three hundred miles out to sea. We were approaching from the Tri-Cities Airport in

Endicott, which was four hundred miles from the ship's location, and our ETA was one-thirty a.m. We were shifting.

With us on the plane, we had two technicians who, at that moment, were fitting me with a suit which they referred to, with that sense of humor that sets nerds aside from the rest of humanity, as the Bat Suit. The one they called Sheldon, and laughed ponderously every time they did so, wore a T-shirt that bore the legend *Eat Your Heart out Area 51* and was explaining it to me.

"This is an exotic material engineered from carbon nanotubes. You can hit it with a sledge hammer, score it with a diamond, do what you like to it, and short of cutting it with a laser, you will not damage it."

I was frowning as he spoke. "So how did you cut it and stitch it?"

He blinked at me like he was having trouble grasping my level of ignorance. "We didn't," he said. "You've heard of three-D printers? Well, these suits—we have three of them—are made with what is essentially a three-D printer, only a very sophisticated one that operates at a nano-particle level."

"So it's bulletproof?"

"It won't protect you from the kinetic force, but it will prevent penetration."

The one with long blond hair down to his waist and an AC/DC T-shirt stepped in.

"However, that is not the purpose of the suit. When you encounter extreme air pressure and spread your arms, the suit automatically deploys the batwings."

"It's basically a wingsuit, a glider suit," I said. "As used in extreme sports."

They looked at each other and smiled a smile that hung somewhere between compassion and amusement.

"*Very* basically. The nature of the material and the design of the batwings means that you have extreme maneuverability, and short of having some form of thrust or anti-grav, you are basically flying. We tested it out at"—they glanced at each other and shared a small, guttural laugh—"at, uh, Indian Springs, and the handling was extraordinary. You'll love it."

I suppressed a sigh. "I believe you."

"In terms of ordnance, we can't offer you anything." It was AC/DC. "Whatever you might have read on conspiracy theory websites, handheld lasers are just science fiction."

Sheldon was strapping a watch to my wrist.

"But this communicator will give you instant video and audio access to the brigadier via a dedicated, secure satellite."

"Is that made of carbon nanotubes too?"

He frowned at me. "Of course."

They both looked at each other and snorted a laugh. "Is it made of carbon nanotubes!"

They snorted some more, and the brigadier emerged from the cockpit.

"You're suited up." It wasn't a question. "You have your weapons?"

I pointed. In the backpack. "My Sig with suppressor, an HK416, spare magazines, Fairbairn and Sykes knife, I'm wearing the Maxim 9, and I have my night-vision goggles."

"Good. If you find her aboard, alert us and we'll move in." I nodded. He watched me a moment. "If you want to abort—"

"No. If you move in with troops and she's not aboard, the whole thing will be blown, and the bastard might get away with a slap on the wrist. Worse, if he makes it to the UK, he'll be protected by Article 2 of the European Convention on Human Rights Act. They take it very seriously there when they're protecting terrorists."

He nodded. "Quite. Are you ready?"

"I'm ready."

Next thing, we were diving and slowing. Sheldon and AC/DC strapped themselves into their seats, and the brigadier hooked me and himself to a bar by the hatch. A red light went on over the cockpit door, and the hatch opened. The brigadier leaned in and shouted, pointing through the hatch.

"*We're at ten thousand feet. That light you see out there is the* Keshti Khoda. *It's about a mile off.*"

I nodded. He slapped me on the shoulder, and I jumped.

I have jumped in a wingsuit more than once but never at ten thousand feet over the Atlantic Ocean, in the pitch blackness of the small hours of the night. I felt the rush of the freezing air on my face, I felt the black void beneath me and the deep blackness of the ocean, and the tiny speck of light in the distance seemed as distant as a star in space. My belly burned. I spread my arms and felt myself slow and rise slightly, and after a moment, I was suddenly possessed by the exhilarating sensation that I could fly. I laughed out loud and began to descend toward the ship.

Soon I could see that it was not one light but several. The ship had a long cargo deck, and at the stern, there was a white tower where the bridge sat over the cabins, the kitchen and dining room, and the recreation area. I angled my arms back slightly to form a delta and accelerated toward the tower. Pretty soon I was no more than a hundred yards behind the churning, slightly luminous foam at the stern of the ship, at a height of no more than two hundred feet above the roof of the structure.

Suddenly the sensation of speed was intense. Before I had been in black space with no real point of reference, but now, with the mass of the ship hurtling at me, I was aware I must have been at a hundred miles per hour minimum, and aside from the risk of a bone-shattering collision, the slightest twitch at that speed could send me careering over the side of the ship and into the black, freezing Atlantic.

I spread my arms wide and curled my body down, as Sheldon and AC/DC had told me to do, and I felt the pressure of the air against my body, braking the speed. I began to descend, and the rushing, surging approach of the ship's tower slowed. I circled it once, slowing further, and finally came to a thudding, sprawling, painful stop on the white expanse of the tower.

And then it was a whole different sensation. From high in the air, the ship's progress had looked smooth and even, plowing through the water. On the flat, steel roof of the stern structure, the sensation was very different. The waves were probably no more than fifty or sixty feet, but a hundred and sixty tons of ship surging, crashing, and corkscrewing through sixty foot waves will hurl a man around some. And with there being no rail or gunwale to hold on to, the prospect of sliding right off into the sea became a real possibility.

The prow of the ship surged in an explosion of spray and rose over a wave, and I began to slide back, clawing with my hands at the slick, steel roof. I swore violently, cursing Sheldon and AC/DC for not having foreseen this, when the prow dipped and plunged into a deep, black canyon of water. I didn't think. I rose on hands and feet and ran forward to the edge of the tower and launched myself into the void with my arms spread wide.

It was a five-story drop. The wingsuit caught the air, and I was instantly drenched in foam as the prow hit the bottom of the trough and exploded. Then the ship was rising to meet me, and I slammed bodily into the steel deck. I groaned, momentarily crippled by the pain, and rolled to the side, aware, even through the agony of the needles piercing my lungs, that somebody on the bridge was bound to have seen a black figure crashing to the deck.

I crawled to the shelter of a lifeboat and gave myself a couple of minutes to regain my breath. It is a golden rule in special ops never to go into a job without exhaustive intelligence, planning, and training. The planning in this case had been land on the roof of the tower, find Beverly, and kill Hussein. Preparation had been an hour with the guys from *The Big Bang Theory*, and the intelligence was lacking everywhere.

But as the pain began to recede, I told myself I was onboard, and two got you twenty Beverly and Hussein-i Sabbah were onboard too, and that was half the task done already. I climbed out of the Bat Suit, and as the huge ship surged and crashed and rolled, I dragged myself to the edge of the lifeboat and peered out toward the tower, where five stories high, the bridge could be seen as a long strip of softly illuminated windows. I thought I could make out a silhouette, but with the movement and the spray, it was hard to be sure.

At the base of the tower, there were two steel doors painted white, and as I looked, one of them was pushed open, and a man stepped out. He was unsteady on his feet because of the roll of the ship, but he was clipped on to a safety cable and was making slow, steady progress to where I was lying, scanning the deck as he went. He was a big guy with swarthy skin and a long, gray beard. He probably thought he was looking for an alba-

THE CELL | 53

tross, but I knew he was looking for me. I didn't want to kill the guy if he was just a sailor doing his job, but neither did I want to be discovered.

As it turned out, he resolved the problem for me when he came around the lifeboat and found me struggling to my feet against the roll of the ship. His eyes went wide, his mouth opened, and he pulled a PC-9 Zoaf semi-automatic from his belt.

I still had the Bat Suit in my hand, and as he pulled the weapon, I lashed out at his wrist with the suit like a whip. It caught his forearm, and for half a second, I paused as his face collapsed in pain and he gripped his arm with his left hand. Carbon nanotubes were good, I told myself. Then I stepped in and drove my right fist into his jaw. His eyes rolled, and I grabbed him by his collar and dragged him in behind the lifeboat. I figured he'd forfeited my leniency by pulling a gun on me. I broke his neck, took his clip and his jacket, and keeping my collar high and my rucksack out of sight, I struggled back to the steel door he had emerged from.

I pulled open the door and stood looking. There was a steel corridor straight ahead that led to another door, and on the right, there was a staircase, though only a few steps were visible, and I couldn't see where it led.

I unclipped myself from the safety cable and stepped in. I let the door close behind me, then staggered to the end of the passage and opened the other door, gripping both sides to keep myself upright. It was a gym with basic amenities and a couple of shower stalls. There was no one there. Hard to do weight training when the floor keeps moving.

I made my way back to the steps. Before climbing them, I took off the sailor's jacket, pulled the HK 416 from the rucksack, and slung the sack on my back. Then I climbed the stairs with the rifle at my shoulder.

I found myself on a landing with a rough, red carpet on the floor. At the end, it made a dogleg to the left, and along the passage there were doors which I figured were cabins. Aside from the grinding shudder of the engines and the sporadic, muffled roar and sigh of the waves, there was silence. It was like the *Marie Celeste* with turbines.

Another flight brought me to an identical, equally silent floor, and the next was almost identical, except that at the end of the corridor, I could see an open door where there were nests of chairs and sofas settled around low tables. There were no people visible, and there were still no sounds other than the creak and grind of the ship and the wash of the sea. It was hard to escape the feeling that either aliens had abducted everyone onboard, or I had been expected and was being led to an encounter where I was going to be outmaneuvered and outgunned.

But the only people who knew I was coming were the brigadier, Sheldon and AC/DC, and the pilot—three besides me and the brigadier. I sighed quietly to myself. It was enough.

I moved down the corridor with my back pressed against the wall, keeping my eyes focused on the common area ahead. At twelve or fifteen feet, I could see a fair chunk of the room but still no sign or sound of people. As I inched forward, the familiar coal began to burn in my gut. At just two feet from the door, I could now see the righthand wall, and at right angles to it, on the far wall, two doors with the WC symbol over them. If there was anyone in this common area, they would be on the left.

Knowing you are about to die eventually becomes second

nature. It becomes a warm, stimulating feeling in your gut and in your lungs. In that moment, I knew I was about to die, but what burned in me was not the will to survive and live but the fear that I would not be able to save Beverly.

I took one large step around the open doors and dropped to one knee with the 416 at my shoulder, and froze. Beverly was there. She was sitting in an armchair. She was not bound, and she was not gagged. She was watching me with absolutely no expression on her face.

SEVEN

I stood and lowered my weapon. She closed her eyes, her lower lip curled in, and tears flooded down her cheeks.

I heard the bathroom doors open behind me and a double footfall. I turned, and there were two guys with standard issue Iranian KLS assault rifles. The WC doors swung closed behind them. Movement where Beverly was sitting made me turn again. Six thugs similarly armed fanned out behind her, and one guy, tall and slim, dressed in black with a pencil moustache and a small goatee stood beside her with his hand on her left shoulder. He said, "You are alone?" I didn't answer, and he said, "You dropped out of the sky. We thought it was a large bird. We didn't expect anyone so soon."

If it had been just me, I might have risked it. I had been reconciled to death for a long time, and if I took this bastard with me, that would be compensation enough. But the risk to Beverly was too high, and it seemed to me in that moment that the last thing she needed right now was to see the guy who'd come to save her get riddled with bullets.

I said, "I thought I'd drop in early, have time for a chat and a drink before dinner."

His face showed no emotion. He held my eye without blinking. "How did you know where we were?"

Any mention of Bella Aurora or *The Woman Who Sailed the World* could cause serious trouble for Beverly. So I said, "You abducted the daughter of a cutting-edge defense contractor. What do you think he makes in his billion dollar enterprise, bows and arrows? We took your undergraduate videos to the lab, found the voice was AI generated, augmented the sounds and images that filtered through the painted window, and tied it all together with satellite imagery." I gave a one-sided smile that was meant to look insolent. "He owns satellites. Did you know that?"

It was hard to read his expression. He ran his fingers through his hair, and I noticed he was wearing black gloves.

"Will you convert to Islam?"

I was surprised, but I didn't show it. I kept the irony out of my voice but said, "Sure. Where do I sign?"

He narrowed his eyes. "Put down your weapons and get on your knees."

It's a kind of golden rule for me. The only time I get on my knees is to take aim. And when I die, it will either be on my feet, on my ass driving some kind of vehicle from hell, or on my back with some woman who is as bad as she is beautiful.

I shook my head. "I will not die on my knees."

"When we get to Rafsanjan, we will discuss how you die."

He glanced at one of the guys behind him. That guy stepped up beside me and drew a long blade that looked razor sharp. There is an exception to every rule. I said, "Take it easy," dropped my rucksack and the Maxim 9 on the floor, and got down on my knees, promising myself as I did so that I was taking every one of those sons of bitches to hell with me.

He looked over my head and gave an upward nod. I heard the footfall behind me and remembered what some guy had told me in the Regiment, that Buddhists believe that your final thought defines your next life.

I tried. I tried to think of peace and love. I even drew to mind a Volkswagen camper van from the Summer of Love, but as the blow fell and blackness closed in, I was promising myself I would not rest until I had returned Beverly to her father and annihilated these bastards.

When I awoke, the first thought that came to my mind was that he must have hit me with an axe and forgotten to remove it afterwards. Because my skull had clearly been split down the middle. Then it began to dawn on me that the pain wasn't just in my head. It was everywhere, but especially in my chest and my lungs. I wondered then if I was in hell and being skewered by demons because there was the hellish noise of diabolical machinery shattering my ears. Reluctantly I opened my eyes and saw that I was in the dim light of the engine room. The pain in my chest was because my wrists had been tied to a pipe running from floor to ceiling. As I had sagged forward, my arms had been trapped at an angle behind me, causing spasms in my back. I struggled to my feet, causing a painful rasping in my lungs, and groaned and gasped as I drew in air.

There was an aisle in front of me between rows of machinery and what looked like turbines. At the end, I saw a man lean in and look at me, then disappear. I closed my eyes and felt with my fingers at the bonds on my wrists. They were not cuffs or zip ties, and it wasn't rope. It was the ever-popular duct tape. Some Mafioso used it in a movie, and now everybody uses it. I don't know why. If you want to make sure a guy is not going to break loose, nothing beats nylon mountaineering rope or wire coat hangers.

I gave myself fifteen seconds to do some controlled deep breathing and, as I finished, I heard the voices approaching. It was Hussein-i Sabbah and two of his boys. They weren't carrying rifles now, only sidearms.

He stopped in front of me, maybe six feet away, and the guy on his right, a big bull of a guy with a big, unkempt beard, came and stood close on my left. Hussein spoke quietly.

"Do you still feel like making jokes about Islam?"

"No."

"Are you willing to convert to Islam and subjugate yourself to God?"

"Yes, but I need your help."

He frowned. "My help?"

"Yes. How will I know I am doing it through true devotion, and not just to escape your torture?"

I thought I'd been smart and given him an answer that seemed sincere and would give me time by engaging him in dialogue. He looked at the guy on my left and nodded once. The guy slammed a fist like a small moon into my floating ribs. The pain was excruciating and made me vomit on the floor at his feet.

Hussein said, "God will know. Subjugate yourself to God. Surrender your soul, your mind, and your body to God. Allahu Akbar."

The two goons echoed him. "Allahu Akbar."

I repeated it, playing up my pain and weakness, though I didn't have to try real hard. " I subjugate myself to the one true God."

"I know you are lying. God knows you are lying. But if you repeat it enough, maybe it will become truth before you die. What is your name?"

"Harry, Harry Bauer. I was with the SAS. I retired. Now I work freelance."

"A paid assassin. We kill for God, you kill for money. You will surely go to hell."

I sagged at the knees, closed my eyes, and shook my head. "I am already there."

"Who paid you to come here?"

"A man. I don't know his name, but he represented Jeff Cook."

He took a step closer, bringing him to within four or five feet. The other goon, a guy in his twenties with a bald head and big brown eyes, closed in and gripped my hair, pulling my head back. It was Hussein who spoke.

"You said technology identified where I was. Jeff Cook's cutting-edge black technology, with all his billions and his infinite technological resources. So I ask you, Harry Bauer, why does he send one man alone, with a rifle and a gun, instead of a fleet of boats and helicopters?"

"He is afraid."

"Afraid of what?"

"He is afraid that if the media and the public get to hear about it, you will be protected by public opinion and human rights activists and politicians, and he wants you dead."

He gave a small laugh of genuine amusement. "So he sends one man alone to kill me. The stupidity of Americans. Don't worry, Harry, I will send you back to Jeff Cook."

"I don't want to go back. I want you to convert me and save my soul."

His eyes told me he was more likely to believe in Santa Claus than me, and coming from a Muslim, that means something. But they also told me he could see a reason for what I'd said.

"You will be punished," he said, "for your crimes against God. Then we will talk, you will prostrate yourself before me and Allah, and then we shall talk about your conversion."

I bowed my head. "Thank you. Allahu Akbar."

He turned and walked away, and they started hitting me, pounding my floating ribs and slapping my face openhanded and backhanders. It's a blow that people laugh at, but well delivered, it hurts and makes your whole head ring and spin.

I had been working, while we were talking, on stretching my fingers up toward the tape on my wrists. Duct tape is great and will hold real tight unless you cut it. Even a small nick will make it split. And I had been working away with my nails. Now as they laid into me, it slowly and painfully dawned on me that even if I managed to nick the tape with my nails, I was too wrecked and too weak to do anything.

I slid to the steel floor, tasting the bile and blood on my lips and in my mouth, and was unable to stand. For good measure, they stamped a couple of times on my thighs, spat on me, and walked away.

As they did so, I raised my voice and called, with more irony than they would ever understand, "*Allahu Akbar!*"

I slept. I don't know how long for, but when I awoke, the corkscrewing of the ship had changed. It was as though we had entered heavier seas. The motion was slower, but the surges and crashes were greater.

During my fitful, painful, almost feverish sleep, I had not stopped working at my wrists, stretching my fingers and my nails up, picking at the tape, and now I could feel the frayed split beginning at the edge. A voice in my head, a voice that was not mine, or no part of me that I recognized, told me it was too little too late. And as I snarled the words out of my mind, I heard a metal door slam. Two guys on unsteady feet appeared, gripping the housing of what I guessed were the turbines, and made their way toward me. I groaned and kept my eyes unfocused. The guy on the left, a young guy with a shaved head, grabbed me by the hair and dragged me to my feet, screaming at me what sounded like "*Baistid! Baistid!*" which apparently in Persian does not mean bastard but stand up.

I groaned pathetically, muttering "*Allahu Akbar! Allahu Akbar!*" as I got to my feet, and then, with a hot, berserker rage exploding in my gut, I ripped the tape around my wrists, gripped the bald guy's ears and rammed my thumbs deep into his eyes as I smashed my instep into the other guy's balls. He wouldn't be making any baistids any time soon. He went down on his knees wheezing and whimpering while the guy with my thumbs in his eyes was screaming hysterically, clawing at my hands. I pulled his PC-9 Zoaf from his holster, shoved him hard at his friend, and they both fell in a heap, where I emptied half the magazine into them.

Struggling to think coherently, I figured either these two had come to give me another going over or, more likely, it was like Hussein had said, first I was to be punished for my crimes against God, and then we would talk. Meaning he would start trying to brainwash me.

So he would be right now either in the common room area or on the bridge. In my mind, I ran over how many men there had been. Two behind me and six behind him, which totaled eight—nine with Hussein. Then there would have been at least a captain and a first mate, making it eleven. Assuming that was all, I had taken out two, which left a total of nine men.

I pulled the bearded guy's weapon and wondered what they had done with my stuff as I made my way toward where I'd heard the door slam.

It was heavy steel, and when I heaved it open, struggling against the pitch and roll of the sea, I saw that it gave into a steel staircase that climbed some seven or eight feet to a small landing, made a hairpin, and continued on up. My body was telling me to just take another ten or twenty minutes to sleep and recover, to get back my strength for what was to come. I reminded my body of what my grandmother used to tell me when she'd wake me at five in the morning: "You'll have plenty of time to rest when you're dead."

I pulled myself up the stairs with every step and every heave corkscrewing pain through my bruises. I turned the U and struggled another sixteen steps to another steel door. There, for thirty seconds, I gave in. I leaned against the wall, gripping the door with my eyes closed, and took three long, deep breaths.

Maybe Odin, Old One Eye, was looking out for me, because the timing could not have been better. I opened my eyes, went through the door, and stepped into a corridor. There, to my left, having just walked past, was a guy with no hair in jeans and a military shirt. He was carrying a polystyrene cup of black coffee which dropped to the floor when I slipped my right arm around his throat and gripped my right bicep, slipping my right forearm across the back of his neck.

I could have squeezed and killed him, but I needed something he might have, so I dragged him back into the stairwell, closed the door with my shoulder, and whispered in his ear, "You speak English?"

He was gagging but managed to nod.

"Where are my things? My suit, my gun, my rucksack —where?"

He pointed up at the ceiling. I loosened my grip slightly. He rasped, "Bridge, captain..."

I pressed hard with my left forearm and tensed the muscles in both arms. His feet scrabbled on the floor, and his hands gripped my arm. I lifted him up. He twitched a few times, then went limp. If my gran was right, he now had plenty of time to rest.

I stepped out into the corridor again, staggered to the stairs that rose to the upper floors, and began to climb.

EIGHT

ON THE WAY UP, I HEARD VOICES IN THE COMMON area: chatter in Persian and laughter. I paused, partly to try and determine how many voices I was hearing and partly to decide whether to take them out before collecting my stuff. I figured I could make out four voices. With the guy I had just taken out of the equation, that left another four, if my calculations were right. That would mean, worst case scenario, up on the bridge I might find the captain, the first mate, Hassan, and one other guy.

Best case was Hassan in his cabin, first mate in his cabin, and the captain and one guy on the bridge. Which, in the state I was in, made that the better option. Not least because in my rucksack, if I was able to recover it, I had an HK 416.

I started climbing again with the question nagging at the back of my mind why the two guys had come down to me. Was it a routine check? Or had Hassan sent them to get me? And if he had, how long before someone went to check on why they hadn't come back? Whatever the case, there was nothing I could do about it anyway, so I climbed the last flight of stairs toward the final white steel door that would take me into the bridge.

I paused for a few seconds on the small landing outside and took some slow, deep breaths. There was pain, I told myself, but I was not the pain. I could dissociate from it. It was there, but it was not me.

I turned the handle at a steady, normal speed, pushed the door open, and stepped in, gripping the jamb to steady myself against the roll and the dip and crash of the prow. I was surprised to see it was dark outside. The captain was seated in a large, leather chair with the light of his display monitors washing his face with blue light. Beyond him, there was a guy leaning into the flame from a lighter, sucking on a cigarette.

It took about two seconds to close the door, brace myself, and take aim. Two seconds is a long time, and the guy with the cigarette and looked up and frowned by the time I punched the two slugs through his chest. They threw him off his chair and sprawled him across the floor.

By this time, the captain was on his feet, staring at me with his mouth sagging open.

I said, "No, Captain, don't do it. It's not worth it. I don't want to kill you. I just want my stuff back. Where is it?"

He didn't answer. He stared at me, then he stared at his controls and then at the back wall, where there were filing cabinets and cupboards. The ship heaved, groaned, and plunged down into a trough, making a vast explosion of foam that washed across the deck and send the captain staggering back against his chair.

"You're a ship's captain. That means you speak English. Now we can do this two ways. I can shoot your knee out and cause you a lot of unnecessary pain. Or you can cooperate with me and go back to your wife and kids in a couple of weeks, when this is all over."

He turned the chair and sat in it, still staring at me. He looked like he might start crying. "How you know I have wife and children?"

I was about to tell him he was a Middle Eastern man in his forties, and the chance of his not having a wife and kids was less than one in a million. Instead I said, "It's in your file, along with your address. Let's not waste any more time. I count to three, and if you're not staggering across the floor to get my stuff, I blow your knee out. With the movement of the ship, I might miss and blow your balls off instead. Is that a risk you're prepared to take?" I did the head-shaking for him and said, "No. Do it. One, two..."

But he was already up, staggering expertly with the pitch and roll of the ship, toward the filing cabinets. He gripped a hold of them, pulled a bunch of keys from his pocket, and unlocked one of the drawers. There he stopped and stood staring down at the contents.

It was written on his face. Most ship's captains are like that. It goes with the territory: courage, commitment, guts. I was about to pull the trigger, but my mouth snuck in first.

"I don't want to kill you, Captain. I'm here to take a young girl back to her father. And I'd like you to get back to your wife and your kids. Be smart."

He showed no expression on his face. He reached into the drawer, and his hand came out holding the wrong end of the Sig. If he'd been holding the barrel, he would have lived, but he was holding the butt, and he had his finger on the trigger. The ship was rolling, and the Sig was all over the place as he tried to take aim. I already had him lined up, and I pumped four slugs into his chest.

It was a shame, but I had no time to regret it. I made a staggering, unsteady run across the floor and slammed painfully into the filing cabinets. I gripped the sides, leaned down as the ship surged over a wave, and recovered my Sig, and as the prow plowed through another huge, rolling wave, I slid down the wall and examined the contents of the rucksack. It was all there. I put the communicator watch on my wrist and slung the pack on my back, struggled to my feet, and turned back toward the door.

There was a guy there. He was frowning. He looked confused. I smiled and said, "Salam," which in Persian means hello, and pointed at the rolling seas outside with my left hand. It takes a little less than one second to say, "Salam," and while I was saying it and pointing, I pulled the Maxim 9 from the rucksack with my right hand. Now he looked alarmed but steadied himself against the door as we plowed into a deep trough. We hit the oncoming wave with a crash, foam exploded around the bows, and I shot him in the left knee.

The ship surged up, and I ran six staggering steps uphill to where he was lying, gripping his bleeding knee with his face screwed up. The sound of his whimpering, like the suppressed sound of the Maxim, was drowned out by the crashing waves. I managed to drag him away from the door and shoved the gun where no man should ever have a gun shoved.

"You speak English?"

He nodded. "Please, don't kill. Pain, much pain."

I nodded. "OK. I won't kill you." I shook my head and wagged my finger. "No kill." I drew my finger across my throat and shook my finger. "No kill. But where is the girl?"

He shrugged his shoulders and shook his head with his face screwed up with pain and fear. It took a fraction of a second for me to decide whether Beverly's life was more important to me than this guy's pain. I put the muzzle of the Maxim on his right knee and pulled the trigger. He screamed, and if I hadn't put my hand over his mouth, it would have been audible over the surge and crash of the sea. I shook my head.

"Wrong answer. I won't kill you, but in the next thirty seconds you'll wish I had. Where is the girl? Girl. Where?"

Now he was nodding and blubbering. "Cabin. Down." He was pointing at the floor and weeping. "Down, one floor, cabin five-teen."

"Cabin fifteen next floor down?"

"Yes, yes, please doctor!"

I stared hard into his eyes. "I go look. Understand?" He nodded. "If you lie, if it's not true, no girl..." I placed the muzzle of the Maxim on his elbow. "Bang!"

He nodded frantically. "No! Is there! Is there!"

It was a judgment call. I figured he would not risk it. I shot him in the head and told myself I was down to seven hostiles. If my calculations were right. For all I knew, there could be twenty guys sleeping. But at an optimistic estimate, I was down to seven.

I got to my feet, pulled the door open, and staggered down the stairs to the next floor. I looked along the corridor and saw rooms thirteen and fourteen. I went past them, being tossed from one wall to the next and back again, keeping my left arm outstretched to the side to minimize the impact. Ahead of me there was what looked like a dining room in darkness.

I paused there to open the door and look in. Over on the far right there were a couple of heavy, swing doors, and through them I could see light. I cursed myself for not having foreseen it. A ship's cook, and how many staff would he have? One? Four? No way of knowing.

I closed the door as softly as I could and made my way around the next dogleg. The first door on my left was fifteen. I tried the handle. It was locked. I waited a moment while the ship creaked and the prow reared up. As it plunged down and exploded into the wave, I shot the lock, pushed the door open, and staggered inside.

Beverly was on the bed. Her hands were tied to the bedstead, and her ankles were tied to the foot. She had a gag in her mouth and was staring at me with wide eyes. I glanced around the cabin.

There was a wardrobe and a chair against the wall. I pulled the chair against the door and moved unsteadily to the bed and pulled the Fairbairn and Sykes fighting knife from the backpack. She eyed it and whimpered.

"I'm here to take you back to your dad," I whispered. *"Take it easy. We'll soon be out of here."*

I cut her bonds, put my finger to my lips, and gently removed her gag. She gasped, *"Who are you?"*

"My name is Harry. Your dad's friend Buddy sent me. Can you walk and run?" She nodded. *"Stay close behind me and do exactly as I say. Got it?"*

She nodded again, and I went and removed the chair from the door. I wedged it open and gestured to her to join me. She came up and gripped my arm. I said, "You OK?"

She nodded. "I do a lot of sailing with my dad."

She gave a tentative, frightened smile, and I returned it on the right side of my face, where it's ironic but encouraging.

I peered both ways up and down the corridor. There was

no one in sight, and I slipped out. She was close behind me. There were no sounds but the sea. The only sign of life had been the captain, his two hands, and the cook. I figured maybe it was late and everyone was asleep.

We came to the corner and staggered past the dining room without being seen, then moved on to the top of the stairwell. There she gripped the banisters while I slid down with my back against the wall, training the Maxim on the corridor below. There was no one there, and I gestured her to follow me, putting my finger to my lips to tell her to be silent.

We took the next three flights like that, one after another, and as we approached the bottom floor, I was beginning to think we actually stood a one in a hundred chance of making it.

I stopped on the bottom step and leaned in to her ear. I whispered, "*We go out on deck. It's rough. I am going to lash my belt to a safety cable out there. You hold on to me, and whatever happens, don't let go. I'll be holding you too. There's a lifeboat thirty feet from the door. We put it over the side and get the hell out of here.*"

She stared at me wide-eyed. "*In this? We'll drown!*"

I shook my head. "*Out there we stand a fighting chance. Those lifeboats are designed for heavy seas. We stay here and we stand no chance at all. You ready?*"

She swallowed hard and nodded. I winked at her and told myself millennials were only as bad as the state school you sent them to. "*Let's go!*"

I stepped down, pulled off my belt, and pushed open the door. I was immediately lashed by freezing wind and spray and staggered as the ship corkscrewed into a wave. The safety cable was maybe six feet to my left. The deck was drenched with water. I took a long step and whipped my belt around the cable. I snatched the end as it came around. The ship lurched, and I fell. I heard Beverly suppress a scream. I still had hold of the two end of the belt and hauled myself back toward the door as the prow of the ship surged and rose. I knew I had just a few seconds, and with feverish fingers I threaded the belt through the buckle and secured it. The ship crested the wave and, with the belt now gripped securely in my left hand, I struggled to my knees and held out my right to Beverly.

She hesitated for just a second, then launched herself at me. She clung to my chest. I gripped her tightly and got unsteadily to my feet. The wind battered us hard, and in an instant, her hair and face were drenched. I shouted at her, "*Grip tight!*" and we started inching our way along the security cable toward the lifeboat.

It was only about twenty-five feet away. In a reasonably calm sea, we could have made it in three or four seconds, but as it was, each step took that long or more with the rise and fall of the prow sending us back three steps out of every four we took and the corkscrewing side to side threatening to throw us to the wet, slippery deck at every moment.

It must have taken us a full minute to get there, but finally we pulled level with the bow, and I bellowed at Beverly over the wind, "*Grab it and pull yourself in!*"

She reached up with her right hand, still clinging to me with her left. I took a step and braced myself against the crane that held the boat and gave her a push. The prow of the ship hit a wave, and spray washed across the ship, blinding me for a moment. I wiped the water from my eyes and saw that she was in the boat. I hollered, pointing at the straps and the life jackets, "*Strap yourself in! Put the lifejacket on!*"

I let go of my belt and hauled myself over the side as she

struggled into the lifejacket. From there, I leaned over the side and hammered with my fist at the winch break and started the lowering mechanism. Grindingly slowly at first with the wind battering us, the boat started to move over the side of the ship with the huge waves swelling beneath us. All that was left to do was to call the brigadier on my wrist communicator and survive until he came to get us.

That's what I told myself.

NINE

WE WERE JUST OVER THE RAIL. ON MY LEFT WAS THE ship. On my right was the ocean. I had clipped myself to the safety cable and was reaching across to secure Beverly. It wasn't easy. The boat was swaying like crazy, and we were being drenched by the spray from the bows of the ship. I had grasped the safety harness and was shouting to her to hold tight when the whole boat juddered to a halt. We hit a large roller as the cold spray lashed us. I ducked down, trying to protect Beverly from being dragged over the side, and I heard the unmistakable whine and smack of a round hitting the lifeboat.

I looked back over my shoulder and swore violently. I couldn't make out how many, but there were men swarming around the winch, and one of them had a rifle trained on me. Then I saw Hussein standing on the platform. The winch started to whine, and the boat started moving back. I pulled the Sig from my belt, planning to shoot Hussein and the guy working the winch, but Hussein produced a megaphone.

"*Give it up, Bauer! Open fire and we'll spray the whole boat.*

I would rather kill her than let her go. There is nothing you can do."

Seconds were passing, and we were already back over the rail. My mind was screaming at me to do something. But every option was the wrong option. Then there were three guys dragging Beverly from the boat. She was screaming and kicking. I reached for her, and the third guy put a gun to her head. I froze. And over the noise of the wind and the spray, I heard Hussein laughing.

"Take a message to Jeff and your masters for me, Bauer! Tell them Hussein-i Sabbah welcomes them to hell! Welcome to hell, Harry!"

With that, the men dragged her from the boat, Hussein kicked the boat release mechanism, the boat dropped, hit the gunwale, tipped, and it and I plunged into the ocean. For long, nightmarish seconds I was in the black, moving silence under the waves. I was attached to the boat by the safety harness. I could feel the vast hulk battering me, massive and heavy between me and the air. I struggled to release myself, but my fingers were numb with the cold, and I couldn't feel the clasp. Then there was a massive, heavy rolling as the boat righted itself and dragged me roaring and gasping from the dark brine and into the air. I coughed and retched as I watched the huge stern of the ship churning away.

A storm of violent emotions raged inside me. I wanted to scream. I wanted to murder Hussein and his men. I wanted to tear them apart with my bare hands. I wanted to weep for Beverly, a tender child whom I had been charged to save and protect, and whom I had failed.

But I kept it all on the inside. A loss of control never saved anyone's life. And though I was pretty sure I was going to hell when the time came, I was damned sure I was going to send Hussein there first.

I knelt in the boat, slipping into troughs and cresting the huge, rolling waves, watching the cargo ship fade into blackness. I wiped the salt water from my face and pressed the communicator on my wrist. The brigadier's crackling voice came back at me.

"Harry! Have you got her?"

I tried to answer, but I couldn't force the words out of my mouth. All I could do was watch the small, receding lights growing more distant with every moment.

"Harry? *Harry?*"

"They threw me overboard." It was a strange voice. It was lifeless and wooden, and I barely recognized it as my own.

"*What?*"

I spoke, but more to myself than to him. "I had her. We were in the lifeboat. But they snatched her and threw me overboard." He was silent. "They are headed for Rafsanjan. You need to send in the cavalry and stop them."

"Are you hurt?"

I lied. "No."

"Someone's on their way to get you. Is Beverly hurt?"

The lifeboat was lighter than the hundred and sixty tons of the cargo ship, so it crested the rolling waves gently, without crashing through them. The wind whipped cold spray off the waves and lashed it in my face.

"Harry? Is Beverly hurt?"

How could I answer that question? How could I define the damage they had done to her? I realized my thinking was irrational and unhelpful and forced my mind to focus. "When I went overboard, she was physically unharmed. But you need to get me to them soon. Every second counts."

He was silent for a moment, and I knew what that meant. I snarled, "Don't even think about it, sir. I am going to get her back if it's the last thing I do in this world. And I am going to kill Hussein and every one of his goddamned men, whether you help me get to them or not."

"Take it easy, Harry."

"You know nobody else can do it. I know who they are, and I know where they are going. You fake my death, and you take me to them."

Harry—"

"*Tell me you'll do it or so help me God...*"

"Yes! Now set a bearing west, leave your communicator on, and try to get some rest. There is a Black Hawk on its way."

I fired up the small diesel engine and turned the boat west, sputtering and puttering over the large, rolling waves, with the wind behind me. I found a blanket and a protein drink and sat and watched the black sky, telling myself a Black Hawk was coming to get me. Weariness moved through me, weighing down on my eyelids and my mind. A Black Hawk, I told myself. A Black Hawk was coming to get me. But how, I wondered as I rose high above the black ocean, if I was the Black Hawk, was I going to get them? I had a message. I was the Black Hawk messenger, and my message was death.

I opened my eyes because I was being blinded by light. The air was glaring and thudding. I looked up and, behind the glare, I could make out the silhouette of the chopper against the sky. I shielded my eyes, and among the glare, I saw a black figure swinging, moving, growing bigger. A guy in a harness with a helmet and goggles was suddenly suspended in front of me. I got unsteadily to my feet on the rolling sea, and he grabbed me. He secured a harness on me, and suddenly we were rising, pulling away from the blackness of the ocean falling away beneath us.

They dragged me into the warmth of the chopper. There were guys in uniform. They were talking, but I couldn't make out what they were saying. I was lying on some kind of bunk, and a woman in uniform frowned into my face and said, "Jesus Christ!"

I tried to laugh but didn't make it to a smile before I felt a prick in my arm, and as I tried to ask her her name, blackness closed in, and I was gone.

———

I AWOKE AND SAT UP.

Dim blue light filtered through an open window. It was tinged by moonlight which made it turquoise. I swung my legs out of bed and stood. Every part of me hurt. For long seconds, I didn't know where I was. Anxiety twisted my gut.

Beverly.

I could see her face twisted with fear as they dragged her away, through the darkness, the wind, and the spray.

A horn outside the window. Far off a siren. I leaned on the windowsill. The Hudson, massive, black, and relentless.

I was at the brigadier's apartment on the Upper West Side. I had failed to get Beverly back. How many hours had passed? How long had I been asleep?

My watch was on the bedside table. I reached for it. Four a.m. I limped to the bathroom, washed my face, and pushed cold water through my hair. I pulled on my jeans and made my way to the living kitchen. I thought about making coffee but grabbed a bottle of beer from the fridge instead. I cracked it and took it to the terrace, leaning on the parapet overlooking Riverside Drive. It was quiet and still. The limpid light made shadows under the trees in Riverside Park.

A footfall made me turn. I'd expected to see the brigadier. I had my mouth in gear to tell him we needed to get out there and stop the ship. But it wasn't him.

She had her hair loose. The city lights and the moonlight reflected on it, giving it golden highlights. She had a blue robe over a light nightdress. She pulled it tighter and crossed her arms as she stood in the doorway, watching me.

"Colonel, I didn't expect you. I thought it was the brigadier."

She didn't answer right away. When she did, she said, "You look terrible."

I tried to smile. "Yeah, that's what my mother said when I was born. Fortunately Hussein's men beat the worst of it off."

She didn't laugh. She didn't even smile. "That's not funny, Harry."

"Tell me about it. I was there. You want a drink?"

Again she didn't answer. There was a round table with four chairs. She crossed and sat, saying, "I couldn't sleep."

"I had her." She glanced at me. "They had me bound in the engine room. That's where they did this." I gestured at my face with the beer bottle. "I managed to get out. I found her, and we made it as far as the lifeboat. We were launching. We were already over the side. But something alerted them."

She watched me move to the table and sit. I went on, "There was no one in the bridge. The whole place seemed to be asleep. But as we were launching the lifeboat, suddenly

Hussein was there with his men. They winched us halfway back over the rail, dragged her from the boat with a gun to her head, and dropped me into the sea." I studied her face for a moment and added, "With a message for Jeff Cook and what he called my masters. Hussein-i Sabbah welcomes us to hell."

She averted her gaze. I watched her a moment and had a growing bad feeling.

"Did you intercept the ship?"

"It was intercepted, but not by us."

"By who?"

"Satellite imagery shows a high speed superyacht. The *Keshti Khoda* was abandoned on the high seas, almost a thousand nautical miles from New York. The analysts say it rendezvoused with a large yacht, the crew boarded that yacht, and it took off doing somewhere between fifty to seventy knots, headed either for southern Europe or north Africa."

"At that speed, they'll make Gibraltar in less than two days. How long have I been asleep?"

"Eighteen hours."

"Jesus Christ! When did the changeover to the yacht take place?"

"About four hours ago. Harry, we need to talk."

"Talk? We don't need to talk, Colonel. I need to get to that yacht."

"No."

"What do you mean, *no?*"

She gestured at me with both hands. "Look at you!"

Her robe fell open revealing a mauve, transparent night-gown. She pulled it closed and shook her head. "You're in no fit state."

"That's beside the point, Colonel. What are you doing about Beverly?"

"We're tracking the yacht and—"

"*Tracking the yacht?* Who is going after her? Who's going to bring her back?"

Her face went hard, and her cheeks flushed. "Keep a lid on it, Harry. The mission was rushed and not properly organized, and it failed because of it. Besides which, this is *not* Cobra's jurisdiction."

"Spare me the bullshit, Colonel! There is a child out there who is going to be raped, tortured, and murdered if we don't do something!"

"Harry!"

"And that will happen while you work out the bureaucratic niceties of jurisdiction and appropriate offices!"

"*Harry!*"

I stared at her, fighting to control the fire in my belly. "What?"

"We *cannot* have a useful conversation if you attack me every time I open my mouth and won't let me finish a damned sentence!"

I sighed, closed my eyes, and sank back in my chair.

"I want to save Beverly as much as you and Buddy do, but we can't do it if we go off half-cocked. So do me the favor of showing me at least the minimal respect you show a man! Shut up and listen!"

I scowled at her. "Fine, but—"

She pointed at me and snapped, "Shut up!" And her robe fell open again.

I raised both hands. "I was just going to say shall we make some coffee?"

"Harry, you have been tortured, badly beaten, and subjected to extreme stress, both mentally and physically. Sending you to extract Beverly would almost certainly cost you —and her—your lives."

"What happened on the ship was not my fault. I didn't slip up. I didn't make a mistake."

"Nobody, believe me, nobody is saying it was. Even Buddy admits the plan was put together too fast without sufficient preparation. You know better than anybody what a risk that is."

"There was no time."

"I know." She held my eye and repeated, more quietly, "I know. This is nobody's fault, Harry. It just didn't play out. So we have to try again, and this time we need to be better prepared."

I leaned forward with my elbows on my knees, fighting hard to control the rage in my gut. "Do you realize what they can do to her while we plan and prepare?"

"Yes. And again, you know better than anybody that rushing in unprepared can cost lives and fail to save the lives you intend to rescue. Harry." She shook her head. "If you had rushed in at Al-Landy, you and your men would have been killed, probably tortured first. And would probably only have served to make those jihadists more vengeful and crueler. It's a truism, but things have to be done right."

I could not hide the bitterness in my voice or in my face. "And doing it right means not using me to bring her home."

She shook her head, as though in disbelief, and gestured at me with her open palm. "Look at you, Harry. You should be in a hospital."

"Bullshit!" I stood and walked to the parapet, looking out

over the trees at the darkness above the Hudson. After a moment, I turned to face her. "Nobody knows these guys like I do. Nobody has the experience I have. Fine, I'll admit we needed more planning and preparation. I'll admit if we go in again, we need to be better prepared. But while we prepare, I can recover and help with the preparation. And there's another thing." I pointed at her. "They will not expect me. Like you, they think I'm done."

TEN

"NOBODY THINKS YOU'RE DONE, HARRY."

I looked up, startled, and saw the brigadier in the shadows by the sliding glass doors. He stepped out in his dressing gown, and I couldn't help looking to see if it matched the colonel's. It didn't.

He stepped out of the shadows carrying a tray of coffee and steaming croissants. He set it on the table and sat so he could look at me where I stood. The colonel started to pour without being asked, and the brigadier gave a small, ironic laugh.

"The only person here who thinks you're finished is you. You're the one who keeps trying to resign. I think you're at the height of your powers."

I was frowning hard, feeling a little disoriented. I felt like a miscreant son talking to his parents. They looked weirdly domestic sitting there laying breakfast out on the table.

"So let me go get Beverly."

He shrugged and sipped. "The colonel is right. You are

badly hurt. The doctor could hardly find a place on your body where there wasn't a bruise. There is a boot imprint on your right thigh. The doctor said it was a miracle the bone didn't break. Won't you sit and have some breakfast?"

I crossed and sat, and the colonel handed me coffee and a hot croissant.

"It's not a miracle," I said. "I have tough bones. I always have. And I recover fast." As an afterthought, I looked at the colonel and said, "Thanks."

The brigadier started to talk, but he had his mouth full, so I got in first.

"I'll go as a cripple," I said. "You can disguise my face with dyed hair and silicon. Give me heavy, horn-rimmed glasses. Put me in a wheelchair."

They had both stopped chewing and were staring at me. The colonel said, "You're insane. You are truly insane."

At the same time, the brigadier said, "How would that work? Talk me through it."

The colonel turned her stare on him and said, "You're both insane. Buddy, we talked about this last night."

"This is an interesting idea, though. Let's talk it through. What is this bespectacled cripple doing in Iran? Are you in Tehran?"

I stuffed half a croissant in my mouth and chewed while I thought.

"She's being taken to Rafsanjan."

The colonel said, "Are you absolutely sure of that?"

"No, I am not absolutely sure. But he mentioned it on the video, and after I told him I refused to die on my knees, just before he had me beaten, he said we would discuss how I would die when we got to Rafsanjan. It was a throwaway comment. So I am pretty sure that's where they are going." I turned to the brigadier. "Rafsanjan is about five hundred miles southeast of Tehran as the crow flies, across desert and mountains."

The brigadier swallowed and said, "The only remotely significant towns between Tehran and Rafsanjan are Yazd and Meybod. Both are run-down, dilapidated, impoverished..." He shrugged. "What possible reason could a Western man, albeit crippled and myopic, have for traveling to either of those places? And I would add, it is not me you have to convince but the Iranian authorities."

He was right, and I nodded. "OK, so I have to start in Tehran and then make my way five hundred miles across the desert to Rafsanjan."

He nodded. "If you were to adopt this as a plan, that is your starting point."

"Then, given that we have to delay to make appropriate preparations, let's set up, in California, the IPSIF." I smiled. "The Institute for the Promotion of Shi'ite Islamic Fraternity. The founder will be Bill Wallace, who has now adopted the name Ali Hassan Moosavi. If Cassius Clay could do it, why shouldn't Bill Wallace?"

"Superfoot."

"That one. Let's get a director in there and make discreet inquiries about building ties with Tehran. Meanwhile, have the Pinedale Roundup announce my passing, along with a short piece on the TV in New York. Man found dead from exposure in lifeboat drifting off Long Island."

The colonel was shaking her head. "You cannot be serious."

She said it to the brigadier. He glanced at her, but I kept talking.

"Once my body has been found, and we are sure Iran knows about it, Jeff Cook makes desperate representations to the Iranian Embassy, and also through secret channels to the Iranian government. He will give them anything they want if they will just return his daughter."

"Yes, that's good, but the IPSIF approach would have to be very low key, almost a formality. The Iranian authorities must not associate the two in any way, shape, or form."

"Agreed."

"Buddy!" It was the colonel. "Sir, Harry is in no *shape* to undertake this mission!"

"You are of course absolutely right, Colonel. However, in the first place, this is *not* a Cobra mission. It is Harry's private arrangement with Jeff Cook. And in the second place"—he turned to me—"if come the time I do not consider you to be up to the job, I will ensure that you do not go. I will not have you killed on a wild goose chase, Harry. And quite aside from that, you must consider that Beverly's rescue is paramount. If you are too badly injured to see it through, for her sake, we must send somebody who is up to the job."

The brigadier and I knew each other very well. I had known him for many years, and he had that English knack of sending non-verbal messages with a completely expressionless face. I knew what he was telling me. He was telling me I had to be in shape and recover by the time we went to Iran, but he was also telling me, "Say yes so she'll stop complaining."

I sighed and nodded. "Of course, that makes sense. But I *will* be in shape. If I'm not, at least I'll have been part of the development of the plan." I looked at the colonel and spread my hands. "Good enough?"

"No," she said, "but I guess it will have to do." Then she shrugged, and there was the ghost of the shadow of a smile. "It is a good plan. We can develop this. But please, Harry, give some serious thought to having somebody else do it."

"I'll think about it."

I said it like I meant it, and she seemed to believe me.

We moved to Cobra HQ outside Pleasantville, and the next two weeks passed grindingly slowly. The brigadier put me in the care of a gang of therapists who controlled how many hours I slept, how much exercise I did, what I ate, and what I drank. The total absence of alcohol was only slightly compensated for by the abundance of first class protein. I managed all of it except the sleep. Whenever I managed to drift off, my dreams were haunted by visions of the girl I had named Miriam weeping with terror and the infinite, incurable sadness in her eyes. And that vision would somehow meld with Beverly being dragged from the lifeboat and the punk holding a gun to her head. His face and Hussein-i Sabbah's were branded into my consciousness, and I knew I would never sleep, I would never rest, until I had put them in the grave and gotten her back home with her father.

The brigadier and the colonel didn't rest either. They set up the IPSIF: The Institute for the Promotion of the Shi'ite Islamic Fraternity and by pulling invisible strings managed to have it recorded as though it had been established five years earlier. So there would be less risk of their associating the small-time organization with Beverly's abduction.

They also had Jeff Cook make official and unofficial representations to Iran begging for the return of his daughter and offering to pay any price and do whatever was necessary for her return unharmed.

It seemed to me that the period of preparation would never come to an end, and the only thing that stopped me spending eighteen hours a day in the gym, beating seven bales of crap out of the sacks was the knowledge that I had to be in shape to see the job through to the end. I couldn't allow myself a pulled muscle or a strained ligament or even a bruised knuckle.

It was on the fifteenth day as I was getting a massage with essential oils of rosemary and lavender beside the indoor pool that the brigadier appeared and politely shooed away my masseuse. As she left with her oils, he threw me a towel and said, "Get dressed. We have work to do."

I sat up. "I'm in?"

"If you're fit enough to be massaged by Mioko, you're fit enough to go to Iran."

"What does the colonel say?"

He raised an eyebrow at me like I was questioning his authority. "I have no idea," he said. "She's in San Francisco, appointing people to the board of trustees of IPSIF. Mostly they seem to be people who drive to demonstrations where they break windows and burn cars to stop us using oil, feminists who support regimes where women are neither seen nor heard, people opposed to racism who believe racism is inherent in certain races, and pacifists who believe violent protest is the only answer." He gave his head a small shake. "Orwell is either sobbing his heart out in whatever version of heaven socialist writers go to or he's jeering at us and shouting, 'I told you so!'"

"This is why I don't read the papers over breakfast anymore."

"You may be wise. They are a sobering reminder that the average human IQ is a mere hundred. Among politicians it seems to be a little less. Shall we go?"

In his office, he dropped into his big, black chair, pulled open his top drawer, and extracted a passport. He handed it to me, and as I opened it, he said, "It's authentic in every regard except that the person displayed in it doesn't exist."

I raised an eyebrow. "Marvin?"

"Don't you feel like a Marvin?" He asked it as he rooted more things out of his drawer. I shook my head. "I'm trying to give them up." He chuckled and handed me an international driver's license.

"We decided against having you confined to a wheelchair in the end. We felt it would inhibit your freedom of movement too much and add another layer of risk to an operation which is already extremely dangerous."

"OK. Makes sense." I held up the driver's license. "What's my excuse for driving inland?"

"You haven't got one." He pointed at his drinks tray by the bookcase. "Pour us a whiskey each, will you? Sit down and I'll explain."

I went to the tray and poured him a Macallan and myself a Bushmills. I carried them to the desk and sat.

He said, "First we are going to fake your death in Tehran. I'll explain how in a minute. The purpose is simply to prevent the authorities from keeping tabs on you. Once dead, you steal a car. We will provide you with plastic, adhesive license plates. The plates will indicate that your car was registered in Meybod. Meybod is south of Tehran, like Rafsanjan, so your car should raise no suspicion driving in that direction. I recommend you go for something hardy but inconspicuous like a Toyota pickup."

I nodded. "Got it. And once at Meybod?"

"Once at Meybod, you are just one hundred and seventy miles from Rafsanjan. A couple of hours' drive. We'll supply you with a desert survival kit—"

"What about weapons?"

"I'll come to that in a moment. So you will drive through Meybod and continue on toward Rafsanjan. However, before entering the town, you will come to the Vali-e-Asr University, and here you will turn left and head north and then east toward the mountains. We'll supply you with satellite photographs and maps indicating the precise location of the training camp. Once in the mountains, you find an appropriate place to hide the car and set up camp. There are abundant caves, canyons, and ravines out there." He gave a small shrug. "After that, find Beverly, kill everyone, and bring her home."

"That's the plan."

"That's the plan. But Harry, I know I don't need to tell you this, but make an example of them. Discourage anyone who might think of repeating the enterprise."

I nodded. "That won't be a problem."

He held my eye. "I don't mean because they targeted a billionaire member of the Military Industrial Intelligence Complex. I mean because they targeted a child." I was surprised. The British military and he never displayed emotion. This was the first time I had ever seen him do that. He went on, "These people are evil, Harry. They attack the weak and the vulnerable, and then they go and hide behind their own women and children. Make an example of them so that next time they will think twice."

For a moment, there was total silence. I said, "I will."

He blinked and looked down at the pile of stuff he'd extracted from the drawer. "Now a few details." He took what looked like a Breitling watch with a brown leather strap and pushed it across the desk to me. "Wear this at all times. It has a direct link to an ODIN Five-Eyes satellite."

"ODIN?"

He looked blank and said, "Mnyuh... You can use it to communicate securely with me and also to take satellite photographs should you need to. One of the nerds downstairs will show you how it works before you go."

"Is this one also made of carbon nanotubes?"

I was being what he called facetious, but he didn't smile.

"I believe so," he said. "Of course the US has no embassy in Iran, but the United Kingdom has a basic skeleton staff in Tehran. Their Secret Intelligence Service attaché there will arrange for your hardware to be provided. I've told him what you will need, and he's making arrangements. He will contact you once you're there and tell you where you can collect it."

"Don't forget to include the gyrocopter and the laser pen."

He looked at me blankly for a moment, gave a small frown, and said, "Laser pens are impossible at the moment. We can't generate the energy in such a small space. But I think you'll find everything you'll need is included."

"When do I leave?"

"Tomorrow morning." He handed me a sheaf of papers. "You are traveling on behalf of The Institute for the Promotion of Shi'ite Islamic Fraternity. You have an appointment with Imam Ammar ibn Ridwan at the Hedayat Mosque on Masjed

Street, in the Ehteshamiye district. Time and date are in the brief. However, you will not make the meeting. You will be mugged and murdered before you have the chance." He cleared his throat. "Your Persian is passable, as I recall, but not perhaps enough to negotiate with a Shi'ite imam."

"That's true."

"Which," he said and sipped his whisky, "brings us to your death."

ELEVEN

TWO DAYS LATER, I TOUCHED DOWN AT THE IMAM Khomeini International Airport, twenty miles outside Tehran. I picked up my Mercedes-Audi-Benz standard Eurocar from Avis and headed into town, where I had a room booked at the Parsian Azadi Hotel, in the north of the city, not far from the mosque where I was supposed to meet Imam Ammar ibn Ridwan at the Hedayat.

Some countries have particular colors. Greenland, in spite of what Eric the Red might have told the Norwegians, is white. By contrast, England, known also as Albion—white—is green. Greece is sage green and turquoise. But Iran is burnt sienna. Iran is the color of singed dirt. Aside from a fertile fringe along the coast of the Caspian Sea, Iran is one vast desert where life itself has lost the will to live.

I took the Imam Khomeini Airport Road into the city. It was an hour-long drive, and all the way, I kept scanning the landscapes to north and south, left and right, looking for something that would alleviate the monotony of brown dust. All I found were paralyzed building sites, desolate high-rise neighborhoods, and that general feeling of despondent resignation that takes hold of places where you are not allowed to step out for a beer in the evening because some guy in a turban and an unkempt beard will have you flogged in the local square.

The human mind is not capable of conceiving infinite space or time. It just goes into overload. So I figure there is no point in my even trying to decide if there is a God. But if there is, I am pretty sure it is way too smart to give a damn if I have a beer or not.

It was a long, rambling drive through a vast, sprawling city of over nine million people. Everywhere there were the signs of neglect, poverty, and quiet despair. This was not the despair of rage and violence and revolution. This was the despair of resignation. Where hope dies in desolation with cynical disbelief as its gravestone.

The apartment blocks were between five and seven stories, and you got the impression that they might have been spacious and comfortable. But except in the most prosperous neighborhoods, the paint was peeling on the walls, cracked concrete remained unrepaired, shops which at that time should have been open had their roller blinds down and covered in graffiti. Each neighborhood I drove through displayed the symptoms of a broken economy spawned by a failed ideology.

I approached on the Yadegar-e Emam Expressway with the Elburz Mountains towering in the north, to my left, a vast wall between the city and the Caspian Sea. I took the exit, wound down more dilapidated, soulless streets, and finally came to the entrance to the hotel. If the city of Tehran was dilapidated and soulless, the Parsian Azadi Hotel was exactly the opposite. Everywhere you looked, there was brass, polished marble, and red carpets. The male receptionists all wore ties and blue jackets, and the female ones were all in gray, with gray scarves over their hair and gray hats over their gray scarves.

The one I spoke to had a four-foot picture of Ayatollah Khomeini scowling at her from the wall behind her. Maybe he could see a wisp of hair poking out from under her scarf that might tempt a few more fallen angels. I offered her a smile and asked her in Persian if she spoke English. She smiled back.

"Of course, how can I help you?"

I gave her my car keys and said, "My car is outside with my luggage in the trunk. My name is Marvin Smith. I have a room reserved."

She called the valet parking to take care of the car, called a bellboy, and signed me in. As I was about to follow the bellboy up to my room, she said, "Oh, Mr. Smith, your friend Pip left a message for you."

She held up an envelope. I took it and followed the kid up to the room. It had an en suite bathroom, a red carpet, and a big window with a view of the mountains. I gave the kid ten bucks and refrained from telling him to have a beer on me. When he'd left, I stood by the window and opened the note.

DEAR MR. SMITH

May I take this opportunity to welcome you to Iran and commend you on your admirable work in broadening and deepening the cultural ties of understanding between this extraordinary country and the West.

I am aware that the United States has no diplomatic mission here at present, so should you need any assistance please do feel free to contact me here at Ferdowsi Avenue. We are always willing to help if we can.

I have kept my diary clear today should you be free for lunch or dinner. Please do give me a call at the embassy to confirm.

Yours Sincerely,
Simon Philips
Cultural Attaché

CULTURAL ATTACHÉ WAS one of the many euphemisms used in intelligence to refer to a counterespionage officer working out of an embassy. I took my cell and made the call. A cheerful woman with a voice that would make a campanologist stop and stare greeted me.

"British Embassy. How can I help you?"

"I'd like to talk to Simon Philips. This is Marvin Smith."

"Hold the line, please. Putting you through."

Philips came on the line after just a few seconds.

"Smith, old chap. Good to hear from you. Free for lunch?"

"I sure am."

"Splendid! Good stuff! Half an hour. Meet you in the lobby."

And he was gone. I had a quick shower, changed my clothes, and made my way down to the lobby. I didn't have to wait. He was at the reception desk as I stepped out of the elevator. He was in a blue suit with an open-necked shirt and had floppy blond hair. He came toward me with his hand outstretched and gave me a good firm shake.

"Splendid to see you, old chap." He slapped me on the shoulder and guided me toward the door. "Anything you absolutely won't eat?"

"As long as it's dead, I'll eat most things. But some things I prefer to eat only in emergencies."

"So lamb broiled with honey and eucalyptus would be all right, then."

"I could manage that."

He laughed as he guided me out through the door to an ancient Triumph TR2 with rounded, swept fenders and spoke wheels.

"My little toy." He pointed at it. "I managed to get the chassis for two hundred quid. The rest of the car had rotted. So I restored it, put a Mustang SVT Terminator Cobra engine in it, putting out about four hundred horsepower, four wheel drive, cutting edge suspension, and it looks gorgeous too."

I lowered myself into the passenger seat and asked, "Does it have an ejector seat for unwelcome passengers?"

He stepped over the minute door and got behind the wheel. "No, that's in the Aston Martin. I thought we'd go to a friend's restaurant in the foothills. The Dost Vafadar, translates as the Loyal Friend." The car growled, and we took off. "He's closed today, but he'll open for me. We might even convince him to open a bottle of wine for us."

It was a fifteen-minute drive through what anywhere else in the world would have been a pleasant, leafy middle-class neighborhood set in a beautiful canyon climbing into the mountains. Here it was little more than a depressing ride through decaying infrastructure and fortified homes set among broken roads, overgrown trees, and vandalized dumpsters.

To say the restaurant was over the top would be an understatement. This was another couple of levels up. By the time we finished winding through backstreets and finally parked, we were no longer on a road as such but a winding dirt track just wide enough for two vehicles. The restaurant had a large, arched gate, and inside the gate there was a tree fat enough for elves to build an entire city in.

Around the tree there were tables festooned with just about anything you could imagine, from potted flowers to silver and brass trays, statues, decorated eggs, and exotic cloths. There were lanterns in the trees, carvings of lions, framed pictures of smiling suns and even a gigantic brass tea urn. It was like walking through a bizarre antechamber to Aladdin's cave.

Philips rapped on the door and glanced at me. "Always reminds me of a Brighton junk shop. Don't suppose you know what that is."

"I lived eight years in the UK. The closest equivalent would be a thrift store."

"Yes, except that in a junk store you get curiosities, antiques, weird things. Not there the lion and the sun. Ah!"

This last was in response to the sound of a key and the big, heavy wooden door being pulled open by a guy the size of a small truck. He had wispy gray hair, blue eyes, and a pale complexion. He flung his arms wide and didn't so much embrace Philips as enfold him in his giantness.

"Simon, Simon, Simon, Simon!" He said this as he pounded him on the back with hands the size of brown bears. He stood back and spread his arms again, laughing. "Naughty man! Only you come when something you want from me! Come! Come! Who is your friend?"

Philips extended his hand to me. "Marvin, I'd like you to meet one of my dearest friends, Darius Spandiyadh, known locally simply as Ali, the greatest chef in Tehran. Darius, my friend Marvin Smith."

We shook, and I noted the keen, analyzing gaze in his eyes.

"You are welcome to my home, Marvin. Come in. I am making lamb. You will never eat lamb like my lamb. The gods fight over my lamb, eh, Simon?"

"They do, for sure."

He spoke as we stepped trough the door and he locked it behind us. The restaurant itself was as cluttered and shambolic as the patio outside. The walls were papered purple and held, at intervals, images of golden lions and smiling suns. Everywhere there were potted palms. The tables were heavy, solid wood, and each chair was different from the rest. In one corner, a log fire burned, and at the far end of the large room, plate glass windows overlooked the abundant trees of the deep canyon, which stood in stark contrast to the harsh, arid mountains that rose above them.

Darius held up both hands and bowed his head to one side. "Simon, Marvin, you will forgive me. I must finish your meal, and then I have things I must attend to. Also I know you have business to discuss. So I will leave you to eat in tranquility. I will join you for a chat after luncheon." He turned to me. "Marvin, I think you are not a Muslim."

"You think right, Darius."

He hunched his shoulders. "I am a damned pagan, so you are in good company with me. So you will have a nice beer to open your appetite, then some good wine with the lamb, huh? And afterwards we can have some whiskey or some cognac."

I gave him a smile on the side of my face where it looks ironic but approving. "A royal name and a royal table."

He pointed at me but grinned at Philips. "You told him?"

Philips shook his head. I said, "Darius is a pre-Islamic name, and the House of Spandiyadh was one of the seven great royal houses of Persia." I pointed at the lions and the suns.

"The lion and the sun, symbols of Persian royalty. You don't do much to hide it."

"Oh, my friend, you are observant. I have royal blood in my veins, but until the return of the kingdom, I must content myself with serving a royal table."

He walked away laughing to himself and pushed through double doors into the kitchen.

Philips pointed to a table in the corner by the fire. "We'll have privacy over there." We sat, and he went on. "Darius, contrary to what you might think, actually keeps a very low profile. He puts up a front for most of his customers as Ali, a true, faithful Shi'ite, but his family was destroyed in the revolution of '79. Most of them were killed. His mother, a woman of aristocratic birth, was spared because she was pregnant, but the price she paid for her life and that of her son was to work, practically as a slave, for a colonel in the revolutionary army."

"So who knows about his true loyalties, aside from you and me?"

"Very few people. Obviously a small group back at the office in London, but even there, you have to be careful these days. The UK is rapidly becoming an Islamic state. It's beginning to feel as though we are racing headlong toward a very serious constitutional crisis."

"Elon Musk seems to have that on his agenda, along with setting up a colony on Mars."

"Let's hope so. Ah, here's our beer."

A young guy with a remarkable resemblance to Darius appeared with a tray and placed two pints of beer on the table for us, then departed with a small bow. We toasted and drank. As I set down my glass, I said, "You have some stuff for me?"

He made a 'hm' noise and wiped his mouth with the back

of his hand. "Well, I haven't. Bit bulky. Chap from your old regiment had it. But he seems to have mislaid it."

I narrowed my eyes. "What?"

"Oh, I wouldn't worry. It's bound to turn up. It's bulky enough. When the old man told me what was needed, I thought he'd taken leave of his senses, but there we are. I passed the message on to procurement, and they sent over a chap with a big pickup truck. He was apparently headed for Meybod or Yazd or somewhere like that but got completely lost. Odd because apparently he knew the area like the back of his hand. But you know what the desert is like."

"Right." I took a pull on my beer. As I set it down, I asked, "So where is he now?"

"God knows." He paused while the waiter brought us olives and nuts to keep us going. When he'd left, Philips continued. "Said it was impossible and what we needed was a coordinated effort."

I arched an eyebrow. "Coordinated."

"Yes, coordinated. How's your memory?"

"My memory?"

"Yes. I have an exceptional memory. Most people don't remember past five years of age. I, however, can remember my father's number plate when I was two years old. You Yanks call it a license plate, don't you?"

I smiled. "My memory is pretty good. Go ahead, what was your dad's license plate?"

"N 31511467. Got that?"

"N 31511467? That's a pretty long license plate."

"Well, that's the North, as it were. My mother's was E 54463326."

"East Anglia? In the East?"

"Yup. Ah, here's the lamb!"

It came up, sizzling in a dense, creamy sauce with the faint aroma of honey and eucalyptus. While Darius served us, his son poured wine from a bottle which I recognized as one of the brigadier's favorites, a Musa 2012 Gran Reserva.

When we were served, he gripped our shoulders in his huge hands. "Enjoy," he said. "And good talk."

They left us to it. I raised my glass to Philips and said, "Here's to a coordinated effort."

BY THE TIME we left the restaurant, after dates, black coffee, and a couple of generous whiskeys, it was closing on four o'clock. We took it easy down the hill.

"I'll tell you what, old chap," he said suddenly as we approached the freeway, "there's somebody at the embassy I'd like you to have a chat with before you head south. He knows that area pretty well and might have some suggestions for you regarding where to hole up, as it were."

I gave him half a smile. "Sounds good to me. Is he the guy who lost my hardware?"

He laughed. "Let's say they are professionally acquainted."

"Right."

We hit the highway, and he accelerated from fifty to a hundred MPH in less than two seconds. After that, if they have a speed limit in Tehran, he broke it by several orders of magnitude. Pretty soon we had arrived at Ferdowsi Avenue and were cruising down toward the big, blue steel gates that enclose the huge British complex.

"It's very convenient having the Russians just across the road, of course. We both get to try out our latest technology on each other. We get to listen to them listening to us listening to them."

As he said it, we pulled up at the gate, and it started to roll back. I glanced to my right and saw he was right. The Russian Embassy, which at eleven hectares was more than twice the size of the British one, overlapped with the British Embassy by about four hundred feet on the far side. As I looked, I noticed a beat-up red Toyota truck pulling away from the side of the road. At the same moment, a sudden movement in my peripheral vision caught my eye, and I looked back at the gate. It seemed to have jammed, and two guys in jeans and sweatshirts were running toward us. I heard Philips swear and reach in his jacket as two more guys beyond him, on the far side of the gate, started running at us.

The whole thing took maybe a tenth of a second. Then the truck was screeching across the road among squealing brakes and blaring horns and had bounded onto the sidewalk, cutting off our access to the embassy compound. Somebody was screaming "*Allahu Akbar! Allahu Akbar!*" I reached under my jacket for my piece. Two guys loomed over me at the car door, point blank range, training their Zoafs on me. A hand gripped my arm, and I felt a piercing pain. Then the two weapons exploded. Blackness enfolded me. I heard Philips shouting, a few explosions, and then nothing.

TWELVE

SIMON PHILIPS, THE CULTURAL ATTACHÉ AT THE British Embassy in Tehran, picked up the secure telephone on his desk and dialed a number in New York. The voice that answered was not American. It was what the English refer to as cut glass. Very English and very upper class. It said simply, "Yes."

"Brigadier Alex Byrd, please."

"Speaking."

"Brigadier, this is Simon Philips of the British Embassy in Tehran."

"Yes? How can I help you, Philips?"

"It's concerning, um, Marvin Smith."

"Is this a secure line?"

"Yes, Brigadier, of course."

"You're referring to Harry Bauer, then."

"Yes. Precisely. We met earlier this morning, and I took him to lunch. We chatted about this and that, as you had requested, and at about four p.m., we drove back. I wanted him to have a chat with someone here at the embassy."

"I think you had better cut to the chase, Philips. What has happened?"

"We were ambushed at the gate, Brigadier. Two men got to within three feet of him and fired eight shots into his chest. I managed to drive through the gates, and we rushed him to the clinic, but he was already dead."

The brigadier was quiet for a long moment. Finally he said, "I see."

"I am sorry. It came out of the blue. They were clearly targeting him. They didn't even try to shoot me."

"He was a close friend of mine. We'd known each other for years."

"You met in the Special Air Service."

"Yes. I was his CO. I'll miss him. He'll be a great loss."

"I'll forward the report to you. What about Rafsanjan?"

"We'll have to abort. There will have to be a consultation. I'll let you know."

"Yes, Brigadier."

"Philips?"

"Yes?"

"Were any of these men known to you?"

"Yes. They were all captured on CCTV. The two men who fired the shots are Afghans who are known to the SIS. The men in the truck and the other two on foot are being processed, but we think they are Syrian guns for hire. The details will be in the report."

"Good. Thank you, Philips. You yourself are all right?"

"I'm afraid so, Brigadier. As I say, they targeted Bauer. Um, there is the question of the body..."

"Have it sent to my address in Pleasantville, will you? Thank you, Philips. I'll be in touch."

Philips hung up and sat staring out at the sprawling gardens for a moment. Then he picked up the phone again and spent half an hour making arrangements for the body to be collected and shipped to New York.

————

SIX THOUSAND MILES AWAY, on Riverside Drive in Manhattan, Brigadier Alexander 'Buddy' Byrd put down his telephone and sat staring at the screen. His face was drawn, and in his belly, he felt the hot burn of anxiety. His jaw hardened, and his lips formed a thin line as he dialed a number in Langley, Virginia. Colonel Jane Harrison answered.

"Yes?"

"Jane, it's Buddy. Are you alone? Can we talk?"

"Yes, I'm in my office. What is it?"

"It's Harry. I'm afraid it's bad news. He's been shot." He heard a sharp intake of breath. "I'm afraid he didn't make it, Jane."

Her answer was a rasp. "*No! Is he...?*"

"I'm afraid he's dead, Jane. He was shot in the chest at close range."

"Who...?"

"It seems to have been a vendetta. The gunmen were known Taliban with support from Syrian hired gunmen."

She was quiet for a long time. Finally she said, "I thought he was indestructible."

"We all did. Including him. He was ambushed outside the British Embassy."

Her voice came slightly distorted. "I thought... We were always fighting. He was insufferable. But I always thought, one day…"

There was a sad smile in the brigadier's voice when he answered. "If it's any consolation, Jane, I think he thought the same."

She said, "What a waste!" and then she started sobbing and hung up the telephone.

The brigadier sat back and stared up at the ceiling. He closed his eyes, puffed out his cheeks, and blew hard, like he was trying to blow his emotions out of his belly, where they were churning and burning.

He picked up his phone and called Jeff Cook.

"Buddy. Any news?"

"Yes, Jeff, there is news, but it's not good."

"What is it?"

"Harry was killed at eight-thirty this morning, four-thirty p.m. in Tehran. He was shot to death outside the British Embassy."

There was an edge of hysteria in Cook's voice. "How? How could that happen? Who knew he was there? This was supposed to be hermetically sealed!"

"It had nothing to do with the job he was on, Jeff. It seems to have been an old vendetta we knew nothing about from his time in Afghanistan. It came out of the blue, and they shot him dead. He was a dear friend of mine."

"I'm sorry, Buddy, but what about Beverly? What about my daughter? What do we do about her now?"

The brigadier gave a helpless shrug that came across in his voice. "I guess you go ahead with what we had discussed. Contact the Iranian Embassy in DC. Use whatever connections you've got to start a negotiation."

"*A negotiation? That could take years!*"

"Do it anyway. I need a few days to see how we can move ahead. We may have to mount a Seal operation, or Delta."

"Jesus Christ!"

"Talk to contacts, Jeff, start the negotiation process. I'll think of something, and we'll get her back."

Jeff made a bitter, almost inaudible remark and hung up. The brigadier rose and went to his drinks tray and poured himself a large Macallan. He raised the glass and spoke softly.

"Odin, All-Father, if any man ever deserved a place in Valhalla, Harry Bauer does. See him safely on his journey. Bring him peace and honor his courage."

And he drained the glass.

———

Precisely six thousand five hundred and eighty-six miles away in the village of Farrokhabad in Iran, a mere ten-minute drive from Rafsanjan, at nine o'clock that night, Hussein-i Sabbah sat cross-legged on a cushion on the floor before a very low table on which he had a very small cup of very strong coffee and his cell phone. It rang, and he regarded it peacefully and yet with a certain malice. His expression seemed to imply that telephoning him was an insolence that might be punishable by death, and his own answering it might be beneath him.

On the fourth ring, he answered it. That is to say he pressed the green button and held it to his ear, but he did not speak.

The voice that spoke to him had an American accent.

"Hussein? I have important information. Are you alone?"

"Yes. What information?"

"The man Cook sent to recover the girl was killed this afternoon—"

"Killed? How? Who by?"

"Zarak Karzai and Behzad Marghai, from Afghanistan. They had some hired guns from Syria. Looks like they had a longstanding feud with the guy."

"What happened to these men?"

"They got inside the British Embassy compound and were shot by the guards."

"Who has the bodies now?"

"The British. But the killing took place outside the compound, in Iranian territory, so the men will probably eventually be handed over to the Tehran authorities." The speaker paused. Hussain said nothing, and the man began to speak again. "I don't know if you've heard from your people yet, but the chatter I'm hearing here in DC is that Cook is pulling strings left, right, and center trying to get a message to you that he will do pretty much anything you ask in order to get his child back."

Hussein smiled, and there was a smile in his voice. "All I want," he said, "is for good men to return to the path of God. I just want Jeff Cook to walk the path of God, of Islam, of subjugation. Nothing more."

"Allahu Akbar."

"Allahu Akbar."

He hung up and rose from where he sat. The house was basic and shabby, with threadbare furniture. He crossed the tiled floor into the primitive kitchen and out through a flimsy door into a dusty yard enclosed by a four-foot stone wall. The yard was big, maybe two acres, and at the far end, fifteen or twenty yards from the kitchen door, there was a low, wooden shack made from old doors and random pieces of timber.

Hussein approached it on sandaled feet with his white robe flapping around his bare shins. He opened the door and had to hunch down to get inside. Inside was a flight of twelve concrete steps that went down into the ground, and at the bottom, there was a small area of maybe nine square feet in front of a green metal door. At head height, the door had a small, steel shutter.

Hussein descended the stairs and opened the shutter. Inside he could see a cell seven foot by seven foot. There were no windows. The walls were cement bricks, and the floor was dirt. There was a bed and a chemical toilet and nothing else save the girl who was lying on the bed.

"Hello, Beverly. I have news for you. Your friend from the ship who came to rescue you. He is dead. He was shot to death this afternoon, in Tehran."

Beverly didn't respond. She lay with swollen eyes and swollen lips, staring at the eastern wall of the cell. Hussein went on.

"But that is good news for you. I have news from Washington that your father is pulling many strings and contacting many people, trying to get a message to me. The message should make you happy." He smiled and let it show in his voice. "The message is that he will do absolutely anything I ask so that he can get his daughter back. If he is telling the truth, you should be back with your father very, very soon."

She heard the shutter slam and the sandaled feet slap up the concrete steps. She curled in, hugged herself, and gave way to violent, spasmodic sobbing, little knowing that in Clearlake, California, her father lay on her bed with swollen eyes squeezed tight, facing the western wall of her room, also surrendering himself to violent, spasmodic sobbing.

Harry Bauer was dead, and all hope was now lost.

THIRTEEN

I awoke on a chesterfield sofa in Philips' office. He was splashing water on my face and slapping my cheeks.

"Come on! As my nanny used to say, 'Get up! You're not dead!'"

I sat up. The room spun three hundred and sixty degrees, and he swiftly handed me a bucket. I vomited copiously. When I was done, he led me to an en suite bathroom, where I splashed water on my face and rinsed my mouth. As I stepped back into his office, he handed me a glass with a milky white fluid in it and said, "Drink it. We haven't much time."

I stared at him, frowned, shook my head, and said, "What the fuck?"

"You're dead. Tonight your body will be flown back to New York. Our chaps have recovered your stuff from the hotel."

I drank the white liquid, and it seemed to settle my stomach some. I put the glass on his desk and sat.

"They were supposed to hit me tomorrow, on the way to the meeting at the mosque. I'm supposed to steal a car..."

I still felt groggy. He sat opposite me.

"Pay attention. Buddy was playing a deep, subtle game because we don't know who is listening in. If Iran has access to Chinese technology, there is no telling how good their listening is, or who might be listening. So he led everyone in Washington and New York to think you were going to get hit tomorrow. This came out of left field, and now everyone except you, me, and Buddy believes you are dead. Including Jeff Cook. As we speak, Cook is going crazy trying to negotiate with Hussein, offering him anything he wants in exchange for his daughter. His guard is not just down. He is totally unguarded."

"I need to get there. I need to get to Rafsanjan."

"Correct."

"I have to get a vehicle. My case, my stuff..."

"Slow down. You're still groggy, and if you try and do anything like this, you'll fuck up, old chap. First a cold shower. Then we get some coffee and protein inside you. Buddy wanted you to steal a four-by-four. But there was no point in that because we already have an old Toyota pickup. We'll put your plates on it, and you're on your way. Don't shave. We've got an old straw hat for you, put a Montana Gold cigarette in the corner of your mouth, and nobody will look at you twice."

"What did you stab me with?"

"Fast-acting narcotic. Don't ask me what it's called. I just know it had lots of PHs and hydro in the name. Something like that. Now go and have a cold shower. I'll arrange some rustic clothes for you, and we'll get you out of here and on your way *fast!*"

I had a long shower, as he suggested, switching from hot to

cold and back again and drinking large amounts of water. When I had dried myself and stepped back into the office, he was not there, but there were some jeans, boots, a scruffy checkered shirt, and a jacket that wanted to look like brown leather but didn't. There was also a box of Montana Gold cigarettes and a box of matches, as well as my Sig and a pancake holster.

As I was dressing, he turned up with a plate laden with a hamburger, bacon, sausages, two fried eggs, mushrooms, and fries. I found I was hungry and cleared the plate without talking while he opened a small, concealed fridge and cracked me a bottle of Doombar ale.

At ten o'clock, I was bundled into the back of a Range Rover with diplomatic plates. Philips took the wheel, and we eased out of the main gate of the embassy onto Ferdowsi Avenue.

At the same time, a large SUV with diplomatic plates and smoked windows also rolled out just behind us. It took off unambiguously toward the airport while we described a couple of figures of eight around the streets nearby and I stared out the back window. After five minutes, he said, "I don't see anything, do you?"

"No. I see nothing. If anyone was watching, they followed the SUV."

"OK, keep watching. I'm going to do a few more maneuvers, then we'll head for Nazi Abad."

"What's that?"

It was hard to make out in the darkness, but focusing on the headlights behind us, I was pretty sure no particular set had stayed on us, and the more twists and turns Philips made, the surer I was we didn't have a tail.

"Nazi Abad," he said after a moment, "is not the abode of the Nazis, where they fled after the war. It's one of the poorer districts of the city. The police kind of avoid the place, and people are pretty laid back there. You see a lot of women dressed normally with no hair covering. People just get on with life. There is a big farmer's market, and at this time of night, the place will be bustling. We have a Toyota pickup parked there, and what we're going to do is park this Land Rover, buy some provisions for your journey, and then you get in your jam jar and I get in mine, and we each go our separate ways."

"Jam jar?"

"Cockney rhyming slang. Jam jar, car. Apples and pears, stairs. Trouble and strife, wife. Here we are."

The place was brightly lit and teaming with people. Aside from the signs over the shops which were mostly in Persian, you could have been at any shopping mall in the West. There were a few women in burkas, many with scarves loosely placed over their heads, but a surprising number were dressed in what we in the West would consider normal clothes, with their hair uncovered, blouses, pants, and skirts. It surprised me, and I said so.

He gave half a laugh. "The grip of the ayatollahs is the grip of mean but weak old men. Though they occasionally have violent spasms and dig in their nails, that grip is slipping. What is going to happen when they lose it is anybody's guess. There's your car." He pointed to a beat-up old red pickup in the parking lot. "It's equipped with a removable GPS to help you get out of Tehran. Once you're out, it's pretty much one road through the desert, all the way."

We climbed out and spent an hour wandering around the street stalls selling everything from socks and sneakers to jeans, fruit, vegetables, and meat. There was also a mall selling cell phones and fashion, and I noticed again that the female mannequins were not displaying burkas but exactly the kind of clothes they might be wearing in New York or London or Paris.

I bought bread and cheese and halal sausages made of lamb, chicken, and beef, plus some fruit and a dozen bottles of water, and Philips helped me carry it to the truck. We stashed them on the floor behind the front seats where they were not visible, and Philips pulled what looked like a radio from the glove compartment. He slipped it into the vacant slot in the dash and slid out a screen. Then he turned to me and held out his hand.

"It's Carplay," he said as we shook. "Just connect your phone by Bluetooth and tell it where you want to go." He smiled. "You have the coordinates, right?"

"Right."

He slapped me on the shoulder, and I watched him walk away into the milling market crowd. A moment later, I swung into the cab of the Toyota, connected my cell, and punched in the coordinates of where I wanted to go. Five minutes later, I, a dead man, a man who no longer existed, was pulling out of the Nazi Abad street market and heading south into the night, out of the gaudy lights of Tehran toward the vast, empty blackness of the deserts of Iran.

IT WAS a six and a half hour drive, and, pretty much as Philips had said, it was one long, straight road through emptiness. Maybe in the light of day, that emptiness would have been striking, even beautiful. But in the night, it was just relentless, empty darkness. Occasionally a gas station would slip by, illuminated in reds and blues and yellows, empty of all but the lonely figure through the window.

Towns slipped by, with names that evoked ancient, angry gods of the desert from before Islam, before Yahweh, before Elohim. Names like Qom and Barzok seemed to evoke, as I sped through that vast night, a time before time, when cruel and vengeful gods still walked among men and demanded sacrifice and subjugation.

Was it so different now?

I passed a sign for Badroud, and something inside told me it was an omen. But good road or bad road, it was the road I was on, and there was no turning back.

By the time I had passed Kashan, I was alone on the road. There was blackness all about me broken only by tiny, distant glimmers that might have been remote villages or stars low on the horizon. Seeing no lights in my rearview mirror or ahead, I pulled over to the side of the road and killed the engine. I reached in back and grabbed the attaché case. From the false bottom, I took the adhesive false plates and climbed out of the truck.

For a moment, I stood transfixed. You are never really aware of the immensity of space or the huge abundance of stars until you go into the desert. It speaks a language we can't hear, about things our minds can't grasp, but still you can feel it, the immensity of it.

I hunkered down and fixed the plates, front and back, took a leak gazing some more at the vastness of the universe, and climbed back behind the wheel. This time I told Siri to play my road trip playlist, and for the next few hours, the Eagles, Creedence, Janis, and Zeppelin kept me company in the darkness.

They were on Badrouds too, I told myself with a smile firmly on my right cheek, and they didn't care either.

At five a.m., as the eastern horizon was turning gray but before it started turning pink, I passed the town of Meybod and started seeing signs for Yazd. And my GPS started telling me there was no road to my coordinates. They were twenty-five and a half miles east of the town, in the foothills of the Yazd Mountains. I had a choice. I could drive through the town and then turn sharp left into the desert, in which case I would have to negotiate the railroad lines at some point, or turn left at the Koran Gate Circus at the entrance to the town, follow the road for three and a half miles into the desert, and then head cross-country to the coordinates Phillips had given me at the restaurant.

Randy Meisner advised me to take it to the limit one more time, so at the Koran Circus, I made a left and plunged at speed into the desert as the sky over the mountains started to turn pink.

After about three miles, the blacktop stopped, and I was racing over beaten earth. Up ahead, I could see a fork in the road with one branch heading straight on and the other turning sharp right into the sloping foothills that rolled away toward the mountains. I slowed and turned.

If what I had been on before was a beaten track, this was just a track, with little to distinguish the yellow-brown dirt of the road from the yellow-brown dirt at its sides. With the mountains now on my left, silhouetted dark against the red and gold of the sunrise, I moved steadily but not too fast. I wanted to avoid raising clouds of dust that might have observers frowning and wondering.

On my screen, I could see my destination as a red pin,

about twenty miles distant, but as I continued following the track, that pin was slipping steadily to my left. In fact, the track seemed to be taking me on a convergence course with the damned railroad tracks again.

I slowed and spun the wheel to my left. There was a big thud and a jolt as I left the path and was now on the bare, open, compacted dirt of the hillside. I guess if I had been unlucky, I might have caused a sand-slide, if such a thing exists, but as it was, the hillside was solid, and aside from the lurching bumps over rocks and potholes, I was able to make good progress at between fifteen and twenty miles per hour. I skirted some of the most bizarre landscapes I had ever seen on my left, promising myself that if Iran ever became a country I could take a vacation in, I would return to this place to explore those mountains.

Up ahead, a large hill in shades of gray, black, and yellow loomed suddenly out of a shallow valley. I figured it was a quarter of a mile away and rose to maybe nine hundred feet. On its eastern side, to my left, it swooped down and rose up again, making a small saddle. And beside the saddle, there was a miniature canyon that was all but invisible unless you were right there to see it. The coordinates Philips had given me at his friend's restaurant sat right bang in the middle of that canyon.

As the sun glowed and peered over the Yazd Mountain tops and turned the sky from icy, desert blue to gold, I ground my way up that hill to the saddle and tucked the Toyota into that canyon. It was no more than three hundred feet long and no more than forty or fifty feet wide at its widest point, with the rocky outcrops and boulders arching in at the top, making it almost a cave. The spot was perfect.

I drove the pickup almost to the end, where it was invisible from above and from the mouth, and killed the engine. The Battle of Evermore died with it, and I sat for a moment in the absolute silence of the rocky haven as the sun inched its way toward the dome.

After a moment, I swung down from the cab and pulled the food and the water from under the back seat. Then I sat in the dirt, ate a small, very basic breakfast of goat sausage, bread, and warm water, and lay down to sleep. It had been close to thirty-six hours since I had slept, and I fell quickly into a deep, dark, dreamless place.

I awoke shortly before midday as the sun peered down into my hideaway and poked me in the eye. The big shadow of a buzzard swept across its brilliance, and I sat up. It was time to dig up the weapons and start killing.

FOURTEEN

HE'D HIDDEN IT WELL. HE'D DUG A HOLE ABOUT three feet deep, placed the hardware inside covered in a canvas sheet, and covered it all with dirt and rocks. If you didn't know what you were looking for, you would have had no idea where to look. But for a guy who did know what he was looking for, and who had been in the Regiment, it was easy. We had ways of letting each other know where things were hidden.

The brigadier had been as good as his word. There were a couple of HK 416s, which is a rifle I like above all for its reliability. One had a telescopic sight and a grenade launcher, the other had a night scope. There was also a Barrett M95. With an effective range of two thousand two hundred yards, its twenty-three and a half pounds in weight could be forgiven. He had also included a Maxim 9 suppressed semi and enough rounds for all the weapons to keep me going for a year.

Aside from the firearms, there was a Fairbairn and Sykes fighting knife. For my money, its design has never been improved upon. There was also a take-down bow with a sixty-five pound draw weight—the perfect balance between power and accuracy—and twelve razor-sharp broadheads. And then the icing on the cake was the fifty pounds of C4 that the colonel would have severely disapproved of.

In terms of non-lethal hardware, there were PVS-14 night vision goggles, a pair of high-powered binoculars, a bunch of detonators, a ski mask, and a field first aid kit.

I examined the stuff, put the sniper rifle in the truck along with one of the assault rifles, the commando knife in my boot, and the Maxim 9 under my arm. The rest of the stuff went back in the hole, where I covered it with dirt again.

After that, I made my way to the top of the hill and spent fifteen or twenty minutes on my belly scouring the landscape. At first, there seemed to be nothing of real interest, but after a while, something caught my attention. It was what looked like a farming community at the foot of a rust-red hill some four or five miles to the south of me. It surprised me because there was no river there, no lake, no apparent source of water. And farming without water is just something you can't do. That's why we have deserts.

As I examined the place in more detail, I became aware first of the road that led from Yazd to Rafsanjan and ultimately to the Gulf of Oman, and then, a little to the south and west of those cultivated fields, a gas station on that road. What struck me about it was that, despite being in such a remote, desolate place, the gas station was big. It was large enough to deal with a bunch of sedans and trucks at the same time. The equivalent kind of place in southern Arizona or New Mexico might have had two pumps and a guy in dungarees to check your oil. This place had two sets of twelve pumps, a big parking lot, shops and a restaurant, and what looked like a motel with a pool. I counted a dozen trucks in the parking lot. You had to wonder who owned those trucks and those sedans, who was shopping and eating in the shop and the restaurant, and who was staying in that motel.

I scanned a little farther to the east and found the ruins of a medieval castle less than a mile from the complex and barely two miles from the farming community. You don't build a castle where there is no water. It's a no-brainer.

"Son of a bitch," I said quietly to nobody in particular. "There's a well down there, an underwater reservoir."

On a hunch, I returned to the gas station and began to examine the desert immediately adjacent to it. My hunch turned out to be right. First I saw the dusty tracks left by trucks joining the road from the desert and exiting the road *into* the desert. And following those carefully, I found a broad, beaten track that led from the gas station up past the castle to the cultivated fields. There, presumably, the trucks would be loaded with fruit and vegetables. But two things argued against that. One was that half the trucks were container trucks designed to carry fluids, not fruit and vegetables. The other was that the beaten track did not stop at the farms. It went on up all the way to the rust-red hill.

"Two'll get you twenty," I told myself, "Hussein-i Sabbah and Beverly Cook are in there somewhere."

But there was more to it than that. I rolled on my back and scowled at the sky. Water, and by the looks of it quite a lot of water, and a farming area that must cover a good nine thousand hectares or more. And trucks, lots of trucks, a few moving farm produce, the others taking liquids up to a mountain in the middle of the desert.

I didn't want to jump to conclusions, but the conclusions

were jumping at me. At the very least, there was unexplained activity at that small, red mountain: There was a demand for food and gas and unidentified liquids which was not justified by the immediate environment.

The colonel would have told me I had insufficient data to draw a solid conclusion, and she would have been right. But the data was sufficient to make an educated guess supported by an intuitive gut. Iran loves its secret, underground facilities. It's the reason Israel is so anxious to get bunker buster missiles from the United States. And my intuitive gut was guessing that Hussein-i Sabbah had brought Beverly Cook to this particular bunker for a very particular reason. And that particular reason involved enough people to require a supply of fresh fruit and vegetables, water, and gas, as well as a supply of what were probably chemicals.

Of course the trucks could be bringing water, but why take it up to the mountain? And why bother putting a nine-thousand hectare farm in a desert without water in the first place? You simply wouldn't. The farms were there for the same reason the castle had been built there a thousand years earlier.

Water.

In the desert, there is one prime motivator that conditions all decisions: water. Once you find water, it has a gravitational pull, and everything else follows. Like castles and bunkers and research and development facilities.

I scrambled back down into the ravine and pulled the maps and satellite photographs from the attaché case. I spread them on a large, flat rock and examined the area. It was a little less than one hundred miles from where I was to Rafsanjan and Sartakht, the two places Hussein had mentioned in his video. Now in retrospect and having seen what I had seen here, it looked like his purpose in mentioning those places was to make it clear to Cook and his advisors that he, Hussein, was a serious player. He wanted Cook to take his threat seriously without giving away the existence of this third facility in the same area. Clearly he had underestimated the combined skill of the Five Eyes, the SAS, and Cobra.

What I needed to confirm now was first that there was in fact a bunker in the mountain, second, what they were doing in there, and third, that Beverly was there. That would have to wait till nightfall.

As the sun went down behind the Zagros Mountains, I would take the Toyota the four miles or so to the proximity of the rust-red hill and park it somewhere among the dunes where it would not be seen. I'd have to get within a mile of the place. The rest of the way would have to be on foot. If I took off at six-thirty p.m., I could be at the hill by seven, allowing for rough, difficult terrain. That would give me some eight hours to do as much reconnaissance as possible. If there was any kind of underground camp or facility there, I'd find it.

I looked at my carbon nanotube watch. In the meantime, I could grab a bite to eat, do some research from space, and get a few hours' sleep. I was going to need it.

I did as much work as I could and got four hours of sleep. At six p.m., as the sun was hanging low over the mountains in the west, I made some strong coffee and packed my rucksack with night vision goggles, the HK 416 that had the night scope attached, and a map of the area and satellite photographs, and for good measure, I packed the Sig and a box of rounds, just in case. The Maxim I had under my arm.

In the darkness of the moonless night, there was little risk of my trail of dust being seen, and in any case, once the sun goes down in the desert, it turns very cold, so there is no warm air to carry the dust to any height. Even so, I took it easy with my headlights off and my speed at twenty-five miles per hour or less.

Progress was slow. Because though with the naked eye, once you get used to the dark, you can see pretty well by starlight or moonlight, through a windshield, you can see nothing unless you have your headlights on. After a mile or so, I realized that my choices were either to drive leaning out the window, stop every four hundred yards to see how I was doing, or blow out the windshield. It was no contest. As the brigadier had said to me once, *"Entia non sunt multiplicanda pra eter necesitatum."* I memorized it so I could annoy people with it when they got on my nerves. Apparently it's called Occam's razor, and it translates as "Always go for the simple answer."

I stopped the truck, put four rounds from the Maxim through the glass, kicked out the shattered spider's web, and slung it in the flatbed. Then I continued on my way with a clear vision of the desert ahead. The simple answer had the added advantage of the cold desert air hitting me in the face and keeping me awake.

As I moved forward across the black sand, ahead of me, the jagged peak where I suspected Hussein had his base began to rise up, a monstrous stencil looming against the desert sky.

At seven-fifteen p.m., I pulled up in the shelter of a rocky outcrop at the base of the small mountain. I shouldered my rucksack and began my approach on foot. Pretty soon, I found myself in a large bowl-like plateau some two or three miles across. Behind me and on both sides, the land rose gradually to a rim above which the sky was a translucent, dark blue, peppered with tiny, frosted stars. Ahead of me, the mountain rose sudden and jagged out of the sand. Now that I was up close, maybe half a mile away, it seemed a lot bigger than it had from my camp.

I kept close to the edge of the plateau and pulled the ski mask down over my face to minimize the vapor from my breath. Then I broke into a jog, ten paces running, ten walking, and began to close on the immediate foothills of what now looked more like a small mountain than a big hill. I found as I went that the ground beneath my feet was compacted and smooth, as though it had been driven over by heavy vehicles.

Pretty soon, the mountain was towering over me, blocking out the stars. In the east, the sky was turning pale, heralding the rising of the moon, telling me I had to seek the shadows and move among them. Directly ahead, the path led to an open expanse that lay between two arms that reached down from the mountain. To my left, the land rose sharply toward a rocky outcrop overlooking the open ground. I left the track of beaten earth and ran steadily up toward the rocks a hundred yards away. There I dropped to the earth and pulled the night vision goggles from the rucksack. I crawled in among the rocks until I was at the very edge overlooking the broad esplanade, and what I could now see was the sheer northwestern face of the mountain.

I scoured the area through the goggles but could see nothing except the clear evidence that there had been activity here. But right now, there was not a truck, not a man, not a light to be seen.

I climbed farther, getting closer to the point where the mountainside became a sheer drop to the flat ground below. I stopped again, lay flat, and scanned the cliff face. Then I saw something.

The moon had started to rise, and there was a luminescence to the air. And now in its strange, turquoise glow, I could see a reflection on the rocks. It was almost metallic, and as I focused more closely, I saw that there was in fact a shelf on what was otherwise a sheer face. It was a broad, flat shelf that disappeared into dark shadow, and it looked unnatural.

I scrambled higher, following the curve of the terrain so that it brought me closer. Again I lay flat and stared through the goggles. Now I could see that where that ledge seemed to disappear into black shadows, it in fact followed a fissure in the cliff, turned out of view, and came back farther down. I kept following it and now saw, as the moon rose higher, that it twisted all the way to the bottom and entered into the flat plateau. It was a road, at the very least a ramp, that led up halfway to the top of the mountain. As works of engineering went, it was a simple task done every day of the year in any opencast mining operation. Here it was an unexplained mystery because it led down to an open expanse of land which showed every sign of frequent use by heavy trucks, and it led up a sheer cliff wall where there wasn't even room for a truck to turn around.

I rubbed my face, pulled the flask of coffee from my ruck-sack, and took a long pull. *Eliminate the impossible*, I told myself, *and whatever is left...* The only trouble was that what was left had to be dumped right into the impossible pile.

I wondered how long it would take me to get down to the esplanade and then climb up the ramp. I figured an hour at least to get there, maybe an hour and a half. It would be a steep climb, and all the way up, there would be nowhere to hide.

I took video and photographs, and just as I was making up my mind to go down and climb the ramp, I saw it. It was minute, and it lasted for a quarter of a second, but there was absolutely no question that I saw it: a tiny wink of light at the very top of the ramp, where it met the sheer rock face.

It was all I needed. There was a skillfully camouflaged door there. We had several of them in New Mexico, and they were good enough to fool satellites and spy planes, and, apparently, crazy guys with night vision goggles. What I had seen was either a flashlight or a side door opening and closing. There was an entrance to whatever camp or facility they had right at the top of that ramp. I rolled on my back, stared up at the infinite sky and the billions of frozen stars, and tried to think.

Doubt set in, but not for long. Any single one of the elements taken in isolation would not be enough to hang any kind of theory on, but all of them taken together made it a cinch. The probability of underground water used for crops and for the ancient castle, the heavy traffic running through the gas station, the fact that that traffic was predominantly liquid containers rather than farm produce, the fact that the vehicles' tracks bypassed the fields and headed for this mountain, the evidence of their frequent passage on the broad, beaten track and on the esplanade below, the broad, engineered ramp that climbed the face of the mountain to apparently nowhere, and finally, that glimmer of light in that very spot where the ramp ended. Taken together, it spelled one thing. There was some kind of bunker or facility there.

But not a bunker as such. As in Afghanistan, large cave systems were not unusual here, and some of them ran deep and sprawling. It would not be difficult, especially with the backing of the Iranian government, to convert a large cave system into some kind of facility. It was known that much of Iran's nuclear research and processing was conducted in that very way. Like I said, Iran loved a hidden, underground bunker.

But even accepting that all that was true—I rolled on my belly and stared down again through the goggles—even granting that I was right about all that, what had driven Hussein-i Sabbah to abduct Beverly Cook and bring her *here?* Why here? One obvious link, I told myself as I watched the motionless darkness where I had seen the glimmer of light, was the fact that Jeff Cook was a defense contractor working at the very cutting edge of computer technology and artificial intelligence. If this facility was devoted to some kind of technological research, perhaps Cook had the technology they were after. That would make Beverly a bargaining tool, not to say a blackmail tool, which made sense.

As I told myself it made sense, I saw another glimmer of light. This time, I was looking straight at it through the goggles, and I saw clearly that it was some kind of a door, and beyond it there was a bright glow.

I lifted the goggles from my eyes and took the HK 416 from my rucksack and looked through the telescopic night scope. Now I could just make out a broad ledge, maybe eighteen or twenty feet across, that came to an abrupt end at the cliff face. But to the left, along the cliff wall, there was an area of blackness, and on staring at it, I began to believe it was a concavity: what had once been the entrance to a cave and was now the concealed entrance to a base.

A microscopic red glow blossomed for a moment and disappeared. I held my breath and waited ten or twelve seconds, and it glowed again before describing a small, descending ark. I smiled. Some son of a bitch was smoking out on the ramp.

"Overconfidence," I told him under my breath, "will get you killed every time."

If I'd had the M95, I might have been tempted to take him out. But there was no point in alerting them that I was here. What small advantage I had right then lay in the fact that they didn't know I was here. Let them be overconfident. Let them continue to smoke on the ramp. Let them relax their guard, right up to the point when it was too late.

I spent another two or three hours exploring the rest of the area to see if I could find any more points of exit or entry. The going was tough and slow, and the temperatures were plunging, making the task difficult and exhausting. So at three a.m., I made my way back to the truck and drove, faster now as I knew the way and dawn was approaching, back to my own cave-like shelter.

There I had something to eat and a long drink of cold coffee and went to sleep as the rising sun touched the horizon with pale light.

FIFTEEN

I SLEPT FOR SIX HOURS AND AWOKE WHEN THE SUN was piercing down from the midheaven causing a slash of brilliance across the floor of my cave-like ravine. I splashed cold water on my face, ate some goat sausage, and scrambled up to the top of my hill. There I spent a couple of hours watching the mountain, where I now knew there was some kind of base or facility. In that time, I saw two trucks climb the track. They were liquid containers painted a dull beige-yellow, and at that distance, they were practically invisible against the desert sand.

They didn't climb the ramp. I waited. After half an hour, I saw movement at the top of the ramp. At that distance, it was hard to see exactly what was happening, but after a moment, the movement resolved itself into an open Jeep moving down the ramp toward the esplanade where the trucks were. It pulled up beside one of the trucks, and two guys in uniform got out. The truck drivers approached, and they seemed to talk. There may have been an exchange of documents, but I was too far away to make it out. Then the drivers returned to the trucks, and behind them, the cliff face opened.

I knew facilities like this existed in the States, notably at places like Groom Lake, where highly classified projects were tested, and I knew that Iran invested a lot of money in exploiting its desert environment to hide nuclear and military facilities, but knowing it is one thing, and seeing it in action is another.

I guessed they had excavated into the side of the mountain, possibly exploiting an existing network of caves, then built in a very large 'garage door' on hydraulic cylinders and painted it the color of the rock face of the cliff. The door must have been at least twenty or thirty feet across and another thirty feet high: big for a door but an invisible speck against the mountainside.

The trucks rolled in, and the Jeep followed them. The door closed.

I lay thinking for a while, staring unseeing at the infinite expanse of beige, yellow, and brown before me. My immediate objective had changed in the last few seconds. Up to that point, it had been reconnaissance: accumulating enough intelligence to take action. That was now no longer the objective. The objective now was to get inside the facility, and the question was how?

That was a difficult question to answer. A golden rule with the regiment was to know the layout of where you are going into like the back of your hand *before* you go in. But there are only two ways to do that. Either you get the plans and as many photographs and videos as you can lay your hands on, or you get inside and have a look.

Neither of those options was available to me. I had to go in blind. And that meant I had to go with plan B. Plan B is that when you are going in blind to a life-threatening situation, you go in explosively and with as much firepower as you can get.

Also, prior to an explosive attack, feint at least once.

The brigadier's words came to my mind. He used to say that the best feint is directed against your most obvious target, because your enemy will be that much more likely to believe the feint is a real attack. His favorite example was a feint to the jaw with your right hand. That will provoke a powerful defensive reaction, at which point you pile drive a left hook into the liver and a straight right into the solar plexus.

I lay with my chin on my hands, staring at the jagged mountain lying across the plain and wondered where its jaw was and where its liver was.

I scrambled back down to my cave, spent a while examining my arsenal, cleaning and oiling where necessary, and in my mind ran through several possible combinations that might get me into the complex without getting me killed the moment I went through the door.

By three in the afternoon, I had come to a decision. I loaded my arsenal into the truck and headed out, real slow in the full afternoon heat, following a roundabout track that for most of the time kept tall sand dunes between me and what I had come to think of as Hussein's Mountain. I made a lot of stops at points where I knew I would be completely invisible and finally came to a halt between two large dunes in the foothills less than a mile from the lower entrance to the facility —or whatever it was.

I loaded my rucksack with the things I was going to need, grabbed the M95, and ran with difficulty through the sand to the rocky outcrop where I had lain the night before. There I sprawled down and put the telescopic sight to my eye, not to stare at the concealed door at the base of the mountain but to check out the gas station in the distance and the large farming area at about the halfway mark. There was no activity that I could detect in either place, and what was more important, there were no plumes of dust moving across the intervening space.

I didn't hesitate. I went over the edge and slid and scrambled the three or four hundred feet down the side of the ledge toward the flat esplanade at the bottom. When I got there, I didn't pause. I sprinted fast toward the face of the cliff where, though I couldn't see it yet, I knew the door was.

I hurled myself to the ground and rolled up tight against the rock face. I lay very still, looking and listening. There was nothing but the glare of the sun and the dust. I scanned the dirt around me and found the tire tracks that seemed to drive up to the cliff and began to inspect it with my fingers. As soon as I touched it, it became obvious, but they had skillfully covered it with exactly the kind of stone irregularities that you would expect, and if you didn't know it was there, you wouldn't see it.

I pulled off my rucksack and took four cakes of C4. Each one weighed one and a quarter pounds, so I was looking at five pounds of highly explosive paste. I spent a couple of minutes pressing the stuff into the space between the door and its frame, making it as compact as I could. Then I stuck in a detonator I had configured to my cell, slung my backpack over my shoulder, and made a run for the ramp.

Through the scope, it hadn't looked like much, but it was a long, steep climb, and by the time I had reached the door in the rock face, my legs were screaming at me for a rest. But there was no time to rest. I had no way of predicting when a truck might turn up or when some guy might step out for a smoke.

The door here was smaller than the one at the bottom. It was set, as I had thought, in a concave section of the cliff. It was about fifteen feet wide and ten or twelve feet high. It was painted the same color as the cliff, but there was no elaborate disguise here. There was no need. It was well hidden from view.

Now I took thirty pounds of C4 from my backpack and packed it in the space between the door and the wall and also on the door itself and the wall where I knew the motor and the hydraulic system would be located. I put in another detonator and ran headlong down the ramp, almost falling off at the hairpin bend near the bottom but managing to make it alive to the esplanade.

From there, keeping in the shadows, I made my way back up the hill to the rocky outcrop on the lip of the ledge. There I lay and rested and drank a couple of pints of water. Finally, at just after five p.m., when life begins to creep back into your average desert dweller, I pulled on my rucksack, grabbed the sniper rifle, and went over the edge again, scrambling down the sandy slope and trying not to leave an obvious track.

Near the bottom, as the slope began to level off, I made my way left toward some boulders at the base of the cliff. There I concealed my hardware. I figured the distance to the big gate at the base of the cliff was some hundred yards. My distance to the bottom of the ramp was just thirty or forty yards, but easily a two or three minute run to the door at the top. Two or three minutes can be an eternity when fractions of seconds can be the difference between life and death.

But that was as good as it got, and that was what I had to work with. The ideal would be for one or two trucks to turn up before six or six-thirty, as the sun was going down. If that didn't happen, my plan went ahead all the same, but if I had the trucks, it was that much better.

As it was, as the sun was almost touching the horizon, I had pretty much given up on the trucks and was about to make my first move when the distant whine of a diesel reached me across the dusk. I reached for the M95, set it up, and peered through the scope. There were two of them, almost invisible against the beige and yellow dirt but approaching at a steady forty or fifty miles per hour. The one on my left was a little farther ahead than the other. They were maybe half a mile away and closing. I could see the driver in the nearest cab. He was a big target with a big moustache. I shifted a little to my right, and I could see the guy in the other truck just as clearly. You can't make judgments about things you don't know, but my gut told me their wives wouldn't miss them much.

I shifted back to the guy in the nearest truck and counted slowly to ten. They were both now in the esplanade and beginning to turn toward the cliff face, a quarter of a mile from where I was. The crosshairs were on his chest, just above his big, spherical belly. I squeezed the trigger and, in my mind, told his wife she was welcome.

His windshield became a spider's web. The truck veered sharply to the right, hit a small dune, over-balanced, and rolled on its side. By this time, I already had his pal lined up. He was turning right to go see what had happened to his friend. I showed him before he got there. I plugged him through his chest. His windshield shattered, and four seconds later, he collided with the other truck. I had three rounds left. I put one into each tanker and wondered what would happen when the hot lead hit the contents. My wildest dreams were fulfilled.

They must have contained some kind of gas, because both tankers erupted in massive fireballs. I watched fascinated as one of the cabs spiraled up into the dusk, engulfed in black and red flames as the dead, burning driver fell from the open door.

I sprang from my place and ran for the ramp, calculating in some intuitive part of my mind how long it would take the guys in the loading bay to get to the door. There was no way of knowing, but my gut told me *now!* And I pressed the detonator on my cell. There was a violent explosion, and the left side of the door was wrenched from its housing.

By that time, I was racing like a hare with a Carolina reaper up its ass up the ramp toward the smaller door. I had feinted at the jaw. Now I needed to drive the left hook deep into the liver. Below me, I could hear wild shouts and screams as I ran. If I had taken them completely by surprise, if I had pulled it off and that gate was what they thought of as their vulnerable spot, I might just make it to the upper door before they opened it.

It paid off. There is no internal, anti-state terrorism in Iran. Nobody goes around shooting cops or placing bombs there. If there is an explosion at a military facility or installation here, the first assumption is that it's a missile, air strike, either from Israel or the United States. So all of their attention was on ground zero, the site of the explosions on the esplanade.

At a hundred yards from the top of the ramp, I stopped, panting, and pressed the second detonator.

Thirty pounds of C4 makes a big explosion. One third that amount will rip a Hummer into pieces. This explosion tore the cliff face apart and created a shock wave that sent the steel door spiraling over the side of the cliff. In its wake came the wailing, screaming, and howling of many voices.

I covered the hundred yards from where I was to the gate in

about thirteen seconds, fueled by adrenaline. I burst through the scorched, shattered entrance with the HK 416 at my shoulder, fitted with the RPG launcher. I was in a concrete tunnel, twenty feet across and maybe thirty feet high. The walls were scorched, and there was a burning Jeep lying on its side. I counted seven bodies. They were grotesque, broken and dismembered, scattered across the floor in an ocean of blood.

The tunnel was maybe seventy or eighty yards long. Any lights there had been were shattered, and the place was in darkness, apart from the dancing orange light from the flaming Jeep. But at the far end, light seeped into the passage through an arched entrance. I ran, splashing through the blood, keeping the weapon at my shoulder. Voices began to echo and roll through the darkness toward me, men shouting. One cried, "*Allahu Akbar!*" as though he was weeping. I kept running. Six then seven silhouettes danced and bobbed suddenly in the luminous arch, running toward me. I could see them because they were backlit. They could not see me. I stopped, dropped to one knee, and fired four grenades at their feet, fifty yards away. Then I closed my eyes and covered my ears.

I felt the shockwaves and the heat of the explosions in the confined space. Then I was on my feet again and running toward the luminous arch just a few yards away, ignoring the charred, twitching bodies at my feet.

SIXTEEN

I was in a brightly lit corridor. To the left, a concrete floor ran past a steel door with a glass panel. It looked like an elevator. Beyond that, I could see the iron head of a spiral, stone stairwell. To my right, the passage ran straight ahead for twenty paces, then made a dogleg to the right. I hesitated a fraction of a second. Which way to go? Before I could decide, two guys came skidding around the dogleg with weapons in their hands. One was a grunt, the other was an officer. I shot the grunt through the head because the officer was more likely to speak English. I shot him in the knee. It bent the wrong way, and he fell on his face, making strange noises of grief, pain, and disbelief. Something inside wanted to feel compassion. But if you abduct thirteen-year-old girls and rape them, you don't get any compassion from me.

I stepped over to him and put the barrel of the rifle against the back of the one knee he had left. I spoke quietly but quickly.

"You speak English?"

"Don't kill me, please. I need doctor. Please."

"We do a deal—make a contract. You understand?"

"Yes, please..." He started to sob.

"You tell me where the girl is. I don't kill you and you get a doctor. You agree?"

I guess if you're desperate enough, you'll believe anything. He said, "Down." He pointed at the stairs. "Down the stairs. Down in the cell."

I put him out of his misery and ran for the stairwell. As I passed the elevator, I heard the mechanism whirring and the creak and grind of the elevator rising. I shot the glass in the door, knocked the shards away with the butt of the rifle, and fired two RPGs down the shaft. Then I ran for the spiral stairs.

It was narrow. The stairs were gray steel and clattered as I took the first steps. Then the whole stairwell shook as the grenades detonated and sent the elevator crashing down the shaft. I kept going, taking four steps at a time. Everywhere I could hear hysterical screaming and shouting. I came to the next floor down. There was a landing. The elevator door had been blown out. A tunnel branched off to my right, and the stairwell lay ahead of me, beyond the elevator. Five men, running, screaming in chaos and waving their weapons came storming out of the corridor. They stopped dead and stared at me. It seemed like a long time, but it was just half a second. I sprayed them with fire in three short bursts, chest height, and made the stairwell beyond the elevator in three strides.

The next two landings were empty of people. There were lots of passages, and I could hear lots of voices shouting. The attack had come as a total surprise to them, and they were gripped with panic. As I started on the fourth descent, I realized the echoing shouts were coming from the next floor down.

I put a fresh magazine in the 416 and continued on down more slowly. When I got to the bottom, I realized it was the loading bay. There was pandemonium. They had barricaded the shattered door, and there must have been seventy men with their weapons trained on the desert. Every now and then they would start screaming at each other. Nearer at hand, standing between two very large trucks, were a colonel, two majors, a couple of captains, and Hussein-i Sabbah. They were all talking and gesticulating at the same time.

The could not see me in the stairwell, and the temptation to take them all out was almost irresistible. If getting Beverly out of there alive had not been uppermost in my mind, I'm pretty sure I would have opened up and peppered the place with RPGs, and the devil take the hindmost.

As it was, I slipped down the last step and moved quietly to the top of the last flight of stairs, into the basement and what the captain had called the cells.

It was the second step that clattered. There was a fraction of a second of silence, and then a shout followed by hysterical screams and a shower of hot lead.

I ducked, felt a graze from a ricochet on my shoulder, ignored it, and returned fire with three short bursts and two RPGs. Then I bolted down the stairs four at a time.

At the bottom, I found I was no longer in a concrete maze of passages but in a stone cave. There were no lights in the ceiling, but arc lamps hung suspended from nails in the walls. I ran.

At first, the ceiling was high enough for me to stand upright, but pretty soon, as I plunged along the passage, it began to drop, and the walls closed in. After a while, I was running hunched over, with barely room on either side to turn if I had to. I knew they had to be behind, and right then, it was just a matter of time before they shot me in the back.

I turned, dropped, and lay on my belly with the rifle out in front of me. I reloaded the RPG launcher and waited.

There was silence and stillness among the heavy stone walls. Gradually I became aware of the sound of slow dripping water. Then, behind that, a soft sighing that I gradually realized was the muffled roar of water.

An underground river.

There was no sign of my pursuers. I was pretty sure I hadn't killed close to eighty men with two RPGs and twelve or fifteen rounds. It didn't auger well. I shuffled back a few feet, listened, heard nothing but the water, got to my feet, and set off at a hunched run again.

After fifty or sixty feet, the ceiling dropped to less than four feet, and the string of arc lights stopped. Had the guy lied to me? Had he sent me on a wild goose chase? I pulled out the night vision goggles, dropped to my belly, and peered into the narrow tunnel. Ten or twelve feet farther on, it seemed to open into a chamber. I knew now why they weren't pursuing me. I was in a death trap. They knew the only way out was through them.

I had two options: go back, kill everybody, and then come and get Beverly or press on and cross each bridge as I came to it. The first was impossible, and the second had no chance of success. For a second that seemed to drag into infinity, I listened to the sigh and rush of the water, which seemed closer and louder now, and on an impulse I didn't understand, I crawled into the tunnel.

I am not claustrophobic, but in that dark, cramped place with the weight of the mountain pressing down on my back, I came as close to panic as I have ever come. I forced my mind to focus on each pull of my arms, and finally I was out in a cavern where cool air stirred and the sound of the river echoed against the walls up into the high ceiling.

I got to my feet. There was very little light, but the goggles made the most of what there was. I was in a passage. The far wall was probably ten or twelve feet away. It was irregular and arched up out of sight into shadows. On my right, there was just a jumble of rocks, but on my left, the walls were smooth and even, like they had been worked by hand. It curved gently to the right. I put the 416 to my shoulder and followed the curve, taking slow, cautious steps.

I came to another chamber. This one was larger, and a faint light glowed from around a corner at the far end. The sound of the water was quieter here, and that made me think. I filed the fact away under 'may be useful later' and continued toward where the soft glow emanated from behind the wall.

I flattened myself against the corner, noted that the wall was wet and stung the graze on my shoulder, and swung around with the weapon at my shoulder. What I saw made my stomach churn, not with disgust so much as anxiety. There was a single arc light on the wall. I lifted my goggles from my eyes, and in the desolate light of the lamp, I could see ahead of me an iron grid set in the rock face of the cave. It was perhaps five foot across and maybe four foot high, describing an arch intersected with iron bars. Through it, I could see rough blankets that looked damp where water was pooling on the floor. Among the blankets, I could see a single pair of very white feet.

I approached and hunkered down. Now I could see the form of a body under the rough blanket and at the end, a tousle of lank, fair hair.

"Beverly?" I spoke quietly. After a second, I saw slight movement of the hair. I spoke again. "Beverly? Is that you?"

The hair moved again, and I saw a pale face looking at me, frowning.

"Who is that? What do you want?"

"It's me, Harry. Your father sent me. Remember?"

She curled her feet in and sat up, rubbing her face. "Harry? From the ship? I thought you'd drowned."

"I'm hard to drown. I've come to take you home."

For a moment, there was no expression on her face. Then she started to say, "How...?" She looked around. "There's no way..."

Next thing she was weeping, biting her lip. Then she covered her face with her hands and started to sob violently. I spoke quietly.

"OK, Beverly, let it out. It'll do you good. You don't need to worry about how. I'll take care of that. I just need you to keep a cool head when the time comes. OK?"

She nodded with her eyes squeezed shut and her hands still over her mouth.

I looked around, wishing I was as confident as I sounded. A few paces from the cell, in the deeper shadows, I was aware of the sound of the water and cool air rising up. As I approached, I was aware of moisture in the air. I stopped dead.

There was a chasm. It was practically invisible until I fitted my goggles. Then I saw that it was wide and deep, and I had been one step from falling in. The far wall was all of twenty feet away. Below, maybe a hundred feet down or more, was a broiling mass of churning foam. I looked to the right and saw, fifty or sixty yards away, a waterfall cascading down a series of jagged rock shelves to plunge finally into this subterranean river.

To the left, all I could see was the same chasm with its sheer, slippery walls, disappearing into blackness. I walked back to the cell and examined the lock on the iron grid. It was a simple, old-fashioned lock with a sliding bolt underneath it. I slid it back and told her, "Get as far back as you can, pressed up against this near wall."

She did as I said. I took the Sig from my rucksack and blew the lock. I pulled open the grate and hunkered down. She crawled closer and gripped my arm with her hands. "Can you get me out? Can we really get out?"

I smiled. "We'll do our best. It won't be easy, but I'm better prepared this time."

It was a lie, but it was a lie she needed to hear if she was going to give it her best shot. I dumped the contents of the backpack on the blanket along with my cell and my Fairbairn and Sykes and told her, "Cover this stuff and shove it over in the corner." I kept the 416 and the Sig and slipped a box of ammo back in the backpack, then told Beverly, "Stay here, don't move" and retraced my steps to the opening of the narrow tunnel. There I slipped the pack inside, like I'd had to take it off to get through, and returned to the cell.

She was sitting outside the cell with her back to the wall. I sat cross-legged next to her.

"How often do they come and see you?"

She seemed to think about it. Her gaze drifted. "It's hard to tell. It's always dark. Every few hours they bring food. Sometimes it seems a long time. Lately I have been sleeping a lot."

"Have they hurt you?" It was a stupid question, and I

sighed and smiled. "I mean, have they beaten you or anything like that?"

She gave her head a small shake. "But I have been very frightened, and the food is just stale bread and water. They said they were going to kill my dad and then me."

I nodded. "They make a lot of noise, but they're not going to kill anybody."

Her eyes said she really wanted to believe me but didn't. "How are we going to get out of here?"

I grinned a grin I really didn't feel. "If I told you, then it wouldn't be a surprise, right?"

She smiled but obviously didn't feel it much either.

"Beverly, I want you to do something for me. The whole rest of your life might depend on whether you do this or not, OK?" She nodded. "I am going to try and get us out of here without having to fight these guys. But if I do have to fight them, I need you to close your eyes real tight and not look. Can you do that?" She nodded like she meant it. I punched her gently on the shoulder. "Good girl."

I had been expecting it, and it came a moment later. It started as the sound of slithering, and then the tread of several pairs of boots. I turned and saw six guys in uniform move in, followed by Hussein-i Sabbah. In his hand, dangling by his side, he had my rucksack.

"There is just you," he said, giving his head a little shake. "You did all this, just you."

"I wish it had done me more good."

He gave a nod. "You are a great warrior. I admire that. But you were stupid to come down here."

I shrugged. "I know, but by the time I realized that, it was too late to go back."

"Mr. Cook was more stupid than you. He has sent you on this mission, but even as we speak, he is negotiating with the Iranian government, asking them to send me a message. He will do anything I want, he says, if I will return his daughter. But he is a snake. Because while he is saying that, he is sending you to cause all this damage. Did he really think he could get away with it?"

I shook my head, smiling at the floor of the cage like he was amusingly stupid.

"Mr. Cook has no idea I am here. After things went south on the *Keshti Khoda*, he vetoed any further attempts at rescue." I nodded at Beverly with my head. "She is everything to him. The fact is, as long as you have her, you own the guy. I set this operation up with my old CO. Cook knows nothing about it."

He stared at me for a long moment. Then he blinked and jerked his head toward the Sig and the assault rifle which were lying next to me.

"Pass over your weapons." His soldiers raised theirs and pointed them at me. "Do anything stupid and you will both be riddled with bullets."

I slid the rifle and the semi across the floor. One of the soldiers picked them up. Hussein said, "And your telephone."

I laughed. "Are you nuts? You think I'd bring my cell on a job like this? It's in my truck, a mile due north of here."

"Stand up."

I stood, and the same soldier frisked me. He gave his boss the nod, and Hussein pointed at the cell.

"Get inside."

I sighed and glanced at Beverly. Her lips were curling in, and she was fighting hard not to cry. I looked at Hussein, like I was appealing to a humanity he didn't have.

"Listen, lock me in that rat hole if you have to, but the girl and her father have cooperated with you. Give her some place where she can at least—"

"Shut up, Mr. Bauer." He said it calmly, took his Glock from his hip, and pointed it at her and then at me. "Get inside."

I put my hand on Beverly's shoulder and gently guided her back in the cell. He closed the door and slid the bolt home. Then he hunkered down and looked me in the eye.

"I'll tell you what we are going to do, Mr. Bauer. We are going to go away and come back in twenty minutes with filming equipment. Then I am going to make a video showing how I force this little bitch to watch as I decapitate you with a blunt kitchen knife. Then I will tell her father exactly what my demands are if he wants to see his daughter again, alive."

He stood and smiled down at me. "Don't go away, we'll be right back."

SEVENTEEN

HE POSITIONED TWO GUARDS BY THE EXIT. I GUESS he thought he should play it safe, in case I chewed my way through the iron bars or punched a hole in the rock wall. Maybe I should have been flattered. As he was turning to leave, I called to him.

"Hussein, hold up a second." He stopped and turned to look at me. "I'm going to die. There is no way I can escape. We both know that. Grant me a dying wish."

He arched an eyebrow. "You want a cigarette? Smoking is discouraged in Iran."

"Come on. Be serious. I don't want a cigarette. I want to know why you are doing this. What's your beef with Jeff Cook? What have he or his daughter ever done to you? Punish me. I'm your enemy. Leave them in peace."

He took a moment to look incredulous. Then he laughed out loud. The echo against the wet stone walls was harsh and ugly. He returned a step, looking at me like I was a mental retard.

"Really? Seriously? You think this childish plea will stop me? It's not worthy even of Hollywood at its worst. You think I am going to do what? Say, 'Gosh, I had never thought of it like that, Harry! You're right. I'll send the girl home right now and let her billionaire defense contractor father off the hook so that he can continue to develop weapons for Israel and the United States, so that they can continue to murder and suppress my people. For my part, I shall vent my religious frustration on you, this grunting, primal killing machine!'" He frowned at me. "Do you realize who I am? I am Hassan-i Sabbah. I am the Old Man of the Mountain! For fifteen years, I have masterminded murder, mass killings, more crimes and terrorism than you can imagine, around the entire globe, in the most absolute darkness and secrecy. Do you really believe your stupid, sentimental plea will move me to anything but contempt?"

"You done? OK, it was a stupid thing to suggest. But what the hell do you want from Cook? You have him over a barrel. Give the girl a room, some clean clothes, some decent food. Cook will do whatever you want him to do."

"Will he?"

"Yes." I said it with real sincerity, and he arched an eyebrow at me. He came and hunkered down in front of me.

"You want to know what I want from him? What I want from him, Harry, is for him to sell his company."

I frowned. "You want him to sell his company? Why?"

His smile was almost lecherous. "Why? Because I am the Old Man on the Mountain, and my mind soars like the eagle. I want him to sell his company so that he can pay me his daughter's ransom." He gave a small, ugly laugh. "This is not your average ransom of a million dollars, Harry. This is a king's ransom. Or to be more precise, a princess' ransom. And to pay that kind of ransom, he needs to be properly motivated."

"A king's ransom? What are you talking about?"

"I am talking about much more than a small mind like yours can comprehend. It's very simple. When he sees the conditions this little pig of his is living in and he sees her face as she watches you decapitated with a kitchen knife, he will do anything, *anything* I say. What will I say? I will tell him that somebody is going to make an offer for the purchase of his company, and he must sell to them. And the money he receives for that sale must go to me, at a numbered account in Panama."

I stared at his face and went cold. Because I knew I was looking at pure evil. "You own the company that will make the purchase."

He nodded. "I do. I own the company that owns the company that will buy the Clearwater Corporation. You see, Harry, Jeff Cook's Clearwater Corporation is a defense contractor not just to the United States, but also, in a disgusting little incestuous tangle, they are also a defense contractor to Israel. The technology that is daily killing my brothers in Gaza, in Lebanon, in Syria, is technology made and sold by Jeff Cook. Did you know he was a Jew? Did you know his little pig wife was a Jew?" He jerked his head at Beverly, who was huddled against the wall fighting tears. "Did you know his little pig daughter was a Jew? And when I own that company, I will own the IDF and all the weapons they use, and nobody will know."

He stood and smiled down at me. "I will own their cutting-edge technology, and when I transfer the manufacturing to

Turkey, Pakistan, and finally Russia and Iran, it will be just a matter of time before Israel is finally wiped off the map."

I shook my head. "Why?" I gestured around me and was surprised at the strength of my own emotions when I spoke. "*Why?*" I said again. "You have some of the richest history on the planet. You have a country that is staggering in its beauty. You have beaches in the south that rival the Mediterranean and the Caribbean. You have oil for Christ's sake!" I could hear my voice rising but was having difficulty controlling it. "From Morocco to Iran, you could have a paradise on Earth! *You don't need to do this!*"

I sagged and sighed and gave myself an internal kicking for my naivety and my stupidity. He leaned close to me, and for a moment, it was like I was looking into the eyes of a snake.

"There are things, you stupid American, that are more important than business, than trade, than making a sacred dollar. This is why you will never understand us. This is why in the end we will get inside you and tear out your hearts. Because you do not know who we are."

"Who are you, Hussein?"

"We are the chosen people of God. Allahu Akbar. Yahya Sinwar said it, but you did not listen. You thought it was hyperbole. But it is the truth. He said our trade is death. We are here to kill you. You make your tourist resorts and trade your oil, American, Jew. We will wait, and we will creep in when you are sleeping or eating or making pig babies, and we will cut your throats. Our trade is death."

He stood and gazed down at me. "And speaking of cutting throats, I must get my kitchen knife and my video camera. I have to make a film."

He walked out, taking four of his guards with him. I

turned and looked at Beverly, listening to the sound of the boots getting farther away. The sound changed as they got down to crawl through the passage. I shifted closer to her. Her eyes were swollen, and I could see pure terror in them. I smiled.

"I'm going to give you a hug, OK? When I do, I want you to close your eyes and not open them till I tell you. Understood?"

Her expression was uncomprehending, but I knew she'd do what I said. I put my arms around her and heard the guards laugh and mutter something in Persian. I slipped my hand under the blanket and came out with the Maxim 9. I whispered in her ear, "*Close your eyes. Don't open them till I say.*"

I pulled back and turned. They were both leering. It was a leer they took to hell with them. I made it smooth and took my time aiming. They were too astonished to react. In two seconds, it was all over.

After that, I worked fast. I reached under the blanket and pulled out one of the remaining cakes of C4. I pulled off a couple of ounces and rammed it under the iron gate where the sliding bolt was positioned just out of reach. I stuck a detonator in and told Beverly, "Get right in the corner. Lie face down. I'm going to shield you."

She huddled up, and I covered her. I pressed nine on my cell, and there was a violent blast.

"Keep your eyes closed."

I kicked the iron grate out, grabbed the two filthy blankets, and threw them over the dead guards. Then I scrambled back into the cell and knelt in front of Beverly, who still had her eyes screwed shut.

"Open your eyes, kiddo," I said. She opened them and

stared at me. "We are *really* short of time. I need to know something, fast. Can you swim?"

She frowned. "Yes."

"Are you a good swimmer?" She nodded. "Good. Stay here. Like the big guy said, I'll be back."

I grabbed the remaining fifteen pounds of C4 and ran for the narrow tunnel. I crawled six feet in and, where the tunnel began to funnel out and expand, I packed the C4 against the wall so that the very funnel shape would provide directional resistance, forcing the blast out, away from the cave and toward the incoming soldiers. I stuck the detonator in, and as I wriggled back out, I could hear the tramping boots and voices approaching.

I crawled out, got to my feet, and walked away three paces. Pretty soon the voices came to me, echoing now in the tunnel. The dancing glow of a flashlight seeped out. I watched it a moment. The voice stopped. The flashlight froze. There was a scream of panic, and I pressed the number nine on my cell.

Fifteen pounds of C4 in a confined space makes one hell of a detonation. Placed as it was so that the tunnel itself acted to direct most of the explosion out, back where they were coming from, it would have been like a cannon, tearing them all to pieces.

"Allahu Akbar," I said quietly and ran back for Beverly.

For a moment, I hesitated. I had taken out seven guys, maybe. That left another seventy topside. I could take the risk of running up the stairs and try to get out and make for the truck. I might make it, but with Beverly in the state she was in, our chances were practically nil.

If there was any way out, and it was a big 'if,' there was only one.

She was standing at the mouth of the cell, wide-eyed, staring at me as I approached. I didn't pause; with the Maxim stuffed in my belt, I scooped her up in my arms and leapt into the void.

Blackness enclosed us. Above the thunder of the water, I could hear her scream ripping through the darkness. It was a timeless moment, and at the center of it was the terrible knowledge that I had sentenced this child to death and there was no turning back.

We hit the water with a painful crash, and suddenly we were beneath the turbulence in a deep, dense silence. I kicked and turned so I was behind her and slipped my arms under her armpits. Then I kicked again toward the churning surface. We erupted from the silence into the thundering, roaring foam. I heard her gasp and shriek at the same time and just had time to fill my lungs before the churning water smothered my face again. I held my breath, struggling to keep her head above the water. I was aware we were accelerating. I kicked, and my head emerged. My heart was pounding, and I was short of breath, but I knew if I drowned, she died.

The water around us was not turbulent now, but the current was stronger and faster. Up ahead, I could hear a powerful hiss and roar. Beverly was screaming, "*Let go! Let go!*" For a fraction of a second, my brain was paralyzed. Then she screamed again, "*It's a waterfall! I can swim!*"

I let go, and we surged. Then we were in midair again, falling through darkness, surrounded by cold, invisible spray. There was silence and stillness that seemed to go on forever. I didn't know if there were rocks at the bottom. I didn't know how far we were falling or if the impact on the water would knock us unconscious and drown us. I knew nothing but the timeless blackness of our fall.

And then the jarring, painful smack when we hit the water. There was a moment of stillness as my whole body smarted with the pain, and I gave thanks to Odin who takes care of lost warriors that there had been no rocks there. I turned this way and that, holding my breath, searching for Beverly. But there was only blackness under the water.

I erupted to the surface and shouted, "*Beverly! Beverly!*"

I heard her gasp, "*I'm here! I'm here! Harry!*" turned, and saw her, pale, almost luminous on the green water nine feet from me. There was light. I swiveled my head, searching for it, and found an ethereal, green luminescence fifty yards away. We were in a pool. There was practically no current, and on either side of us, there were rocky banks. But ahead, a hundred or a hundred and fifty feet away, there was an arch, like a tunnel, and through it a faint light was glowing.

We struck out for the shore. The water was icy cold, and as we pulled ourselves out, she was trembling and so was I. Some part of my mind was telling me that our most immediate problem now was that she was going to go into shock, and in the freezing temperatures of the desert at night, she could get hypothermia. I grabbed her hand and said, "Beverly, run! *Run!*"

I pulled her, and we started to run for the stone arch where the water was spilling out of the cave. After three steps, she was pulling on me, dragging back like a lead weight. This was what I had most dreaded: that she'd cave in and collapse when I most needed her to respond. I turned back, intending to sling her over my shoulder and carry her out of the cave, and I stopped dead in my tracks. She was bent double, supporting herself with her hands on her legs, staggering. Slowly she went down on her knees.

Weak, helpless with laughter.

EIGHTEEN

FOR A MOMENT, I FELT A SPASM OF ANGER. I HAVE seen too much death—and worse—to find it something to laugh about. But as she covered her mouth with her hands and looked up at me, my anger drained away. She got to her feet and staggered toward me as the laughter, born of sheer relief and disbelief, turned to tears. She flung her arms around me and began to sob violently. I held her and told her it was OK, and we were going to get out of that place and get home, and she would be safe, and in my mind, I could see that place in the Wind River Mountains, where Freemont Creek tumbles out of the snowy peaks and tumbles into a deep canyon on its long journey toward Freemont Lake. I could see that indescribable view which seems to defy gravity and makes you believe that perhaps, after all, you have a soul, and that soul can rise above the hell that is this world and fly.

And I saw Miriam's eyes—that girl I had named Miriam— to whom I had promised freedom from the hell visited on her by men who claimed for themselves the supreme jurisdiction of God's will.

I wept from my soul, trying to hide it from Beverly, but the pain felt as though it were being pulled out of my physical heart by its roots. It was a matter of just a few seconds, and I blessed the freezing water for the multitude it concealed as I stepped back. I wiped my face with my sleeve and told her, "I hear you, but we haven't got time for this now. Every second counts. Let's go!" She nodded, wiping her eyes, and we ran.

We came to the big arch that formed the mouth of the cave. Through it I could make out the light of the moon reflecting on the surface of a small lake.

"Wait here. I'll check it out. If we're clear, I'll call you."

She nodded again, trembling with cold, and I slipped into the water. I struck out and swam the nine or ten feet under the arch that led to the outside.

Above me was a vast, sweeping dome of translucent night sky transformed almost to turquoise in the light of a vast full moon. On my right, the rock face curled down to a rocky beach that lay some thirty feet away, and on my left, the lake opened out in a great curve. At the far end, straight ahead of me, the shore was two hundred yards away, and from what I could make out, the water was drawn away into a stream or a canal.

The cold of the water was biting into my limbs, making it hard to move and to breathe. I swam back into the arch and called to her, "*All clear! Dive in and swim hard to the right. There's a beach.*"

She dove in, and we both swam hard, splashing through the dark water. Fortunately, the beach was close, and it quickly became shallow enough to stand. I don't know how long either of us would have survived in that temperature. As it was, in the freezing desert night, we were looking at hypothermia if we didn't warm up soon.

We stumbled out across the loose stones and rocks and onto the soft sand. She was hugging her arms as she walked, but I didn't let her stop. *"Run!"* I grabbed her elbow and dragged her along. *"Run! Ten paces running, ten paces walking! Ten paces running, ten paces walking! Count them as you go! One, two three..."*

As we ran and walked, I scanned the hills around us, trying to orient myself. I began to realize we had come out at the rear of the mountain. It had to be because I had seen the mountain from the north, the east and the west, and there had been no sign of a lake or a stream. Plus being in the south put the rising moon on my right, which was correct.

"At a rough reckoning," I told Beverly, "my truck is a mile across these dunes. If we're lucky, it will still be there. We'll get you warmed up and fed and work out a way out of here."

She didn't answer. She just kept walking and running, looking at her feet, and I wondered if she was going to make it. I was pretty sure she wouldn't, and the dilemma facing me then was, did I carry her for a mile through the sand, or did I leave her and bring the truck to pick her up?

After half an hour, I was half-carrying, half-dragging her along. Shock had kicked in, not to mention several days of surviving on stale bread and water, and the cold was beginning to get inside her. Her legs were failing, and I was thinking we were going to have to stop and rest. But I knew if we stopped, the cold would get inside her, and then we would have a serious problem.

I had been focusing so hard on keeping her on her feet and

moving that I had stopped observing our surroundings. But now, as she slid to her knees, I glanced around and knew where we were. I heaved her to her feet. "Just a little farther, Beverly. Just a little more. You see that crest? Twenty feet away, seven long steps, that's where the truck is."

She stared, swaying, said, "Come on, seven steps" and passed out.

Picking up a hundred and ten pounds as a dead weight in the sand is not easy. Somehow I managed it. *Seven paces*, I told myself as the sand gave way under my feet. Six paces, then five. I ignored the cold and the exhaustion that came with it. I pushed one step after another and came to the brow of the hill. Below me, exactly where I had left it, was the truck. I staggered a couple of steps down, lost my footing, and we both fell, rolling down through the soft sand.

I got to my feet, went into a stumbling run, and reached her as she came to rest by the front wheel. I pulled her up, wrenched open the passenger door, and somehow managed to bundle her in the passenger seat. There I splashed water on her lips, and she started to come around. I slammed the door, ran around the hood, and climbed behind the wheel. I was beginning to hear the whine and roar of diesel engines, and I could see the glow of headlights in the distance around the mountain.

I pressed a button on the side of my carbon nanotube watch and said, "Harry Bauer, find my location."

A voice that was somehow both female and robotic said, "I have you pinpointed, Harry."

"Red imperative one. Call in bunker buster strike for WMD site."

"Acknowledged. Recommend you abandon site immediately."

"No kidding."

I fired up the engine, put it in reverse, and hit the gas. But it was too late. As I came to the bottom of the dune and spun the wheel to head north toward my refuge, the area was flooded with the light from twelve powerful headlights. Four were directly ahead of me. Four were on the dune behind me. There were two on my left and two on my right. And I had one very wet Maxim 9 with which to blast my way out of there. We were badly screwed.

There is only one thing you can do. When you are surrounded by six four-by-fours loaded with an untold number of men whose prime motivation in life at that moment is to kill you, there is only one thing you can do. You fix your eyes on the guy directly in front of you, and you play chicken. I snarled, "Strap in, get down, and don't look" and hit the gas.

I went straight for him. The plan wasn't as crazy as it seemed. At first there was a hail of lead that hit the cabin and caused no damage at all because I was hunched low and they were aiming for me, not for the engine or the tires. But as I drew closer to the trucks ahead of me, the guys behind me and to the sides had to hold fire in case they hit their pals. Plus, they still wanted Beverly alive if they were going to make Jeff Cook pay a king's ransom for her. So I hit the gas and roared like a maniac toward the truck in front of me.

There was one more thing that counted in my favor. Two got you twenty whoever was driving that truck had a lot more to lose than I had. He swerved when he was seven or eight feet away. If he thought I was going to plow straight on and try to escape, he was wrong. Not a lot of people know this, but you are a damned sight safer in a head-on collision than you are if you get struck from the side. It's all about the design of your spine. Your vertebrae can cope a lot better with head-on whiplash because you're designed to bend forward and backward. Severe lateral whiplash will tear your vertebrae apart and destroy your central nervous system. So as he swerved violently to his left, I swerved violently to my right and rammed him with the bull bar.

It was a pickup, and I saw the four guys in the back go flying as it skidded and rolled on its side. Whoever was in the driver's seat and the passenger seat had gone to cash in on their seventy-two virgins. I reversed in a shower of sand, spun the wheel left, and plowed through the guys who were sprawling in the sand. I don't know how many I hit, but the truck bucked and thudded at least four times.

There was chaos behind me. Headlights were playing across the sky like lighthouses on speed. In my rearview mirror, I saw three trucks almost collide as a fourth stopped to help the truck I'd rammed. I roared ahead, took off over a sand dune, and crashed down in a massive cloud of dust. I didn't stop. I kept going, retracing the roundabout path I had taken to get here. In my rearview and side mirrors, I could see a string of headlights following me. I couldn't make out how many.

Beverly scrambled up and knelt on her seat, gripping the sides with her arms, looking out the rear window. "There are four," she said. "I think one stayed behind." She hesitated a moment. "My dad's in the RNA. He taught me how to shoot when I was four."

"No."

"Give me the Maxim."

"No way!"

"I have a right to defend myself. I have a right to fight for my life. There are at least twelve men out there who want to kill you and rape and torture me before killing me. Give me the Maxim."

I swore violently under my breath and handed her the gun. As I skidded around a dune, she scrambled into the back of the truck. In my mirror, I saw her brace herself on the back seat with both arms extended out in front of her.

"Slow down a little and keep a straight course for a few seconds!"

The response was automatic. She was right. I slowed, held the course steady, and heard four rapid cracks behind me. As I hit the gas again, I saw in the mirror how one of the vehicles swerved violently and the truck behind it rammed it and over-turned it.

I rounded another dune, and they were lost from sight. The one I had ahead of me was low, and I knew we were near my base. I shouted, "*Hold tight!*"

I plowed over the crest, left the ground, and belly flopped on the soft sand on the other side. The engine whined, and we roared onto the path again.

"*Are they on our tail?*"

"*No!*"

"*Are you OK?*"

"*I'm fine!*"

Two minutes later, the truck scrambled up the hill too fast, and somehow I managed to get it into the cave-like ravine without tearing it apart. I killed the engine and jumped down without pausing, ripping off my shirt. I shouted, "*Stay where you are! Don't move!*"

I ran down to the slope outside the entrance and started beating at the dirt like crazy with my shirt, obliterating the tire tracks that led up to the mouth of the cave, otherwise almost invisible from below. Just over the hills, I could see the dancing beams from the headlights. I sprinted back up the hill, grabbed the cloth that had covered the weapons, and wrapped Beverly in it. I put my finger to my lips, placed her in a small nook behind the hood of the Toyota, and returned to the flatbed. There I grabbed some items and stashed them beside the entrance to the cave, where they could not be seen. Finally I took up a position behind some rocks where I could cover the entrance.

For the moment, nothing happened, and there was silence but for the distant hum of diesels. They were searching for us. I pulled my cell and called the brigadier.

"Harry."

"I'm sending you my location. I have Beverly. I have called in a strike. We are hidden in a kind of cave in the desert, but we have three trucks searching for us. Maybe twelve men or more. I think Hussein is dead, but I cannot be one hundred percent sure yet."

"All right, listen. Three F-16s were scrambled from the Gulf just off Kuwait half an hour ago. That's about four hundred and thirty miles. They should be closing in imminently. Stay put. I'll have them take out any vehicles roving in the dunes."

I hung up. I could hear the trucks louder now. They were going slowly. I saw the glow of headlights pass the entrance to the small ravine. They stopped, and I heard a second truck stop. There were voices. Then shouts. I trained my weapon on the entrance. They hadn't found the tracks leading to my hideout, but they had seen where my tracks stopped suddenly. It was what I had feared, but there was damn all I could do about it.

The question now was, how many men was I up against? They had lost two out of six trucks. One at least had stayed behind. If I was lucky, there were three trucks outside with at least four men per truck.

That was if I was lucky.

The voices were approaching. They were excited and shouting, and in a bizarre way, they reminded me of little boys at school when they form a gang and get high on bullying a weaker kid.

And then they were filing into the cave. There were twelve of them. Two of them were holding up a grotesquely disfigured Hussein. His face was burned on the right side. He seemed to have lost an eye, and his right arm was badly scorched. They all stared at the truck. Hussein's face seemed to twist like a burned fist, and he screamed, "*Harry! Harry Bauer! Give me my girl! She is mine! Give her to me and I will kill you quick!*"

They stood staring around in the silence. There were murmured exchanges. They thought maybe we had left on foot. Hussein shook his head.

"*I know you are here! There is no escape for you! There are troops on their way. The police are alerted. I will kill you in such pain and so slowly you will beg for death!*"

His voice echoed among the stone walls. Maybe it was stupid of me. I could have taken him at any moment. But I wanted him to know. I wanted him to take the knowledge to hell with him that his mountain fortress had been destroyed.

The scream was sudden and tore the sky apart. They ducked reflexively and ran out of the small, narrow ravine to watch. I counted twelve explosions. They shook the ground as the bunker busters penetrated deep through the rock and blew the tunnels, the passages, and the cell to hell.

Seconds later, two of the jets screamed overhead. As they banked and turned, Hussein and his men came scrambling in, screaming and shouting, seeking shelter from the deadly jets.

I lined Hussein up and plugged a 9mm through his forehead. The back of his head erupted. He looked surprised, like he was about to say, "You did *what?*" His guys stared at him, frowning. The Maxim 9 had been inaudible under the scream of the F-16s. They were approaching again. Hussein was sinking to his knees. His men were looking around them like they didn't know which side death was coming at them from. That was when one of them saw the four fuel containers I had stashed by the entrance. I'll never know if they saw the detonator I had stabbed into one of them. I pressed nine on my cell, and as the F-16 shot the hell out of the rigs parked outside, the gas containers exploded in a ball of swirling fire that enveloped the men. They danced and screamed, and I took them out with eleven shots, not out of vengeance, but out of compassion.

NINETEEN

I FOUND MY BAG OF CLOTHES AND THE PROVISIONS. I
had taken them out of the truck before setting out for the facility. I took them over to Beverly, who was shivering and
sobbing. I prayed silently that she had not seen what had
happened. Hearing it was bad enough.

I took a towel, some jeans, a sweatshirt, and a sweater from
the bag and handed them to her with a couple of pairs of socks.

"Dry yourself and put as many warm clothes on as you can.
They'll be too big for you, but they'll keep you warm. And eat.
You need to eat, even if you don't want to. I'll make some hot
coffee. You rest, try and sleep."

She watched me without expression as I spoke. I handed
her what I had left of sausage and bread and, while she changed
her clothes, I made a fire and put some coffee on to brew.

My phone rang.

"Harry, it's me, Buddy. What's your status?"

"Hussein is dead. Confirmed beyond doubt. The facility

they had has been destroyed, and the men who were pursuing us are also dead. All of them. Beverly is in shock, and I worry about hypothermia here in the desert. I have her by the fire now in warm dry clothes and eating. Before he died, Hussein said he had called for reinforcements and had alerted the cops. I don't know if it's true, but we need an extraction, fast."

I heard him take a deep breath. "The risk of entering Iran airspace right now, after the strike, is too high. You need to find a vehicle, if you haven't got one already, and head south to Bandar Abbas. Put the girl in a burka. Have you grown a beard? Try to look inconspicuous. In Bandar Abbas, head for the Haghani Marina. Somebody will meet you there with a boat. Keep me posted. I'll be in touch."

I gave Beverly an hour to warm up with hot coffee by the fire and to sleep. Meanwhile, I dragged the charred corpses out into the sand, took their keys and what cash they had, and buried them as well as I could. Then I had a look at their trucks. There were three of them. Two had been torn to shreds by the F16s, but the third, which had been partially behind the hill, was more or less intact. It at least had a windshield. I tried a couple of the keys I'd taken and managed to fire it up. I figured it would do to get us to Bandar Abbas. It would be an eight-hour drive through the night, and if we set off soon enough, we might even avoid the cops.

I checked the fuel gauge. It had a quarter of a tank. I had no idea where the next gas station would be, so despite the risk, we would have to gas up at the station outside town, the one near the farms. It would be a big risk but one we had to take.

I took the adhesive plates from my truck and put them on the new one, then went and woke Beverly. She looked ill.

"We have to go," I said, "before they start looking for us."

She nodded, but it was a moment before she was able to stand. I filled a flask with fresh coffee and led her out of the shelter and helped her into the passenger seat. I got behind the wheel, and we rolled away from the small canyon cave. I headed north first, toward the town of Yazd, though it seemed counterintuitive. My thinking was that a truck rolling out of the desert into a gas station at night was going to attract attention. I wanted to lose us among the populace of the town. And I was also thinking that the brigadier had been right. I needed to get a burka for Beverly in short order.

I could pass for Iranian. There are plenty of tall, fair-skinned Iranians with blue eyes. But not so many driving a truck at night in the vicinity of an air raid with a young girl in the passenger seat who had California written all over her from head to foot. But where the hell do you get a burka at close to midnight in the middle of the Iranian desert?

The answer presented itself unexpectedly. As we approached the town from the northwest, retracing the route I had followed on the day I had arrived, I began to notice that there were huge crowds in the street, and they were all looking south and east, in the direction from which we had come. I slowed, looked back, and smiled. The colonel would be proud of me.

The mountain where Hussein-i Sabbah had had his base looked like a volcano. Huge flames were issuing from the top and in spouts from the cliff faces, among roiling black clouds of smoke. The scene was oddly silent. I had no idea what they had been working on or what they had been developing, but whatever it was, it was clearly highly flammable.

But more important than that right then was that it had everybody and his grandmother out on the streets, gathered at the intersection and in the squares. And if they were on the streets, that meant the houses were empty.

As we approached the Koran Gate Circus, I pulled over to the side of the road. There was no sidewalk. It was just dirt, but set back from the road was a house. It was surrounded by a seven-foot wall and had a steel gate. But the steel gate was open, and I could see a fat guy in slippers and a dressing gown standing at the corner among a crowd of neighbors. They were all staring agog at the burning mountain in the distance. I observed him for a moment. He had with him what looked like his mother-in-law, his wife, his wife's sister, and four kids of varying ages. It was anybody's guess, but I didn't think there could be anybody else left in the house. I turned to Beverly.

"Stay down, out of sight. I'll be back in a couple of minutes."

Her voice came back small and afraid. "Where are you going?"

I gave my head a small shake. Thee was no time for explaining. "Stay out of sight," I said. She hunched down under the dash. I climbed out, locked the truck, and slipped in through the steel door to the house.

There was a front yard with abundant palms and banana trees. I moved through it and found the front door open. I stepped inside with the Maxim 9 in my hand and found myself face to face with a woman in a burka. I guess in a house in deepest Iran, that should not have surprised me, but it did, and for a moment, we both just stood and stared at each other.

The shift and sway of the burka told me she was drawing

breath to scream, and I reacted. I shoved the Maxim in her face and put my finger to my lips. She froze. I searched the Persian phrasebook in my memory banks and said, "*Labasato dar biar.*"

I hoped it meant, "Take your clothes off," and by the gasp she let out, I guess it did. I repeated it with more aggression, and she started to weep as she pulled off the burka. Underneath that ugly cloth, she was a pretty girl with a nice face and a good figure. She was trembling and about to drop the robe on the floor. I took it in my left hand and, as she started to undo her underclothes, I shook my head. She frowned.

I said, "*Lazm nist. Lazm nist.*" It wasn't necessary. Then I added, "*Moteshkaram, khodahafez,*" thank you and goodbye. I even gave her a small wave and a smile.

She was looking at me like I was crazy, and I was debating putting her lights out to stop her screaming for help when she turned and ran into the house. I followed, thinking she was going to raise the alarm. She burst through a door, and I stopped dead. She was at a wardrobe, pulling out another burka and slipping it over her head. She stared at me a moment, then waved me away.

The logic of it dawned on me. I smiled at her and said, "*Shma besiar ziba npastid.*" I hope I told her she was very beautiful and not that her mother was a camel. I guess I'll never know, but judging by the smile she gave me, I got it more or less right. I ran back to the truck. It was just in the nick of time. As I slammed the door and shoved the burka on top of Beverly's head, the fat, greasy guy in the dressing gown turned and started making his way back toward the house with his extended family trailing behind him.

Rape can mean a death sentence in fundamental Sharia law. Not for the rapist, but for the woman he rapes. Even if it never gets to the judges, the woman's husband or father can make her existence a living hell. I pulled away from the roadside and moved slowly toward the Koran Gate Circus while Beverly struggled into the burka. What that girl back at the house had realized instantly, and I had been slow to understand, was that if she told her father or husband or whoever the guy was that a foreigner had been in the house, held her at gunpoint and taken her clothes, rape would probably have been assumed. At the very least, having been seen half-naked by another man—and a Westerner at that—her life from that point on would not have been worth living.

She did the smart thing. She let me take the burka and sent me on my way.

I glanced at Beverly. "Suits you," I said. "You look like a Christmas tree in mourning."

She might have smiled. I couldn't see, but after a minute, she said, "I won't tell you what *you* look like."

"If I look half as bad as I feel, I'm surprised you're still conscious."

I drove through the town nice and slow. The streets were overflowing with people, but there wasn't a cop in sight. The only sign of any military was a chopper that appeared and started searching in a grid pattern over the desert to the east of the burning mountain. Beverly sat motionless beside me in complete silence.

It took about fifteen minutes to get through the town and start moving through the suburbs. As we did so, the glow from the fire became more intense, reflecting in wavering orange and gold off the building and the faces of the crowds who stood staring at it. Twenty minutes after that, we were approaching the gas station, with the burning mountain looming close and the chopper, now joined by a second one, crisscrossing the hills and the dunes looking for us.

I had a half-second hesitation. My instinct was to drive on by and get the hell out of there. But two things argued against that. First was that I didn't know how far it was to the next gas station. Second was the fact that by stopping, filling up, and driving away, we would attract less attention than simply driving past. Stopping and gassing up right there was the last thing you'd expect a fugitive to do. So I did it.

I have basic, phrasebook Persian, and I wanted to avoid risking any conversation. So again, the temptation was to pay by card at the pump. But then again, looking at the state of my truck and the state I was in, I was struck by doubt. Do Iranians living in the desert wilderness pay for their gas with credit cards? Would anyone notice?

I opted for the risk, shoved the card in, and filled her up. I kept an eye on the window. The kid behind the counter was talking to his pal. Nobody would notice the transaction for hours, possibly days. Maybe never. I settled the hose, removed my card, and made for the driver's door.

I heard the shout as I reached for the handle. I paused and looked across the hood. It was a cop. He'd pulled up outside the store and was shouting at me, striding across the forecourt rattling something I didn't understand and pointing at my truck. Two got you twenty he thought he'd recognized it. Maybe it was his cousin's truck. He went to the back and stared down at the plates. I thanked the gods they were filthy. That truck with brand spanking new plates would have been bad news. He looked at me and shouted something. Acting on a flash of inspiration, I pointed at the pump and spoke like my tongue was missing, or I was a mute. I said, "*Tazeh par kardam*," which means I just filled up, but I made it sound like, "*a-eh ar hanang.*" Then I pointed down the road and for good measure added, "*Ang a-ang I long*," which should have been "*Man alan mi rom*," or I am leaving now.

He peered at me through narrowed eyes. I saw his partner get out of his vehicle, staring across the forecourt at us. He shouted something, it might have been this cop's name, because he turned and looked back at him. He didn't say anything but turned back and stared at Beverly through the window. I could feel the Maxim heavy in my waistband behind my back. I said, "*Fansa ang.*" *Npamsar man* would have meant 'my wife.'

He scrutinized me again and drew breath. His partner yelled at him and gesticulated for him to get back there. They had a damned infidel terrorist to catch. My guy ran his eyes over the truck, said something that sounded obscene, and returned to his partner. With a scorching of tires, they were out of the gas station, fishtailing left onto the highway and screeching back toward town. I rolled carefully out and turned right onto the highway like I was as bad at driving as I was at enunciating. I accelerated steadily until we were at the speed limit of seventy miles an hour, scanned my mirrors, and gave a deep sigh.

Then I looked at Beverly. She was watching me from tired eyes. "How're you feeling?"

"Tired, a bit better, thanks." Her voice was sleepy.

I smiled. I put my fingertips and thumb together like an Italian chef and said, "Ee-nun-see-ate! Eee-nun-see-ate!"

She laughed.

"Like me," I told her. "Didn't you hear me? How I *ee-nun-see-ated*? Now oddy ownah unnershtan you if you oan't ee-nun-see-ate!"

She was laughing loudly now, and it was a beautiful sound to hear. I laughed too, and we drove on into the night with just three hundred and fifty miles to go before we reached the coast.

TWENTY

SHE SOON FELL ASLEEP AS THE DESERT SLIPPED BY IN darkness. My body ached all over, from my scalp to the soles of my feet. Inside, the ache of exhaustion was deeper still, but there was a different ache. An ache that would not let me rest, however tired I was, until I saw Beverly back with her father. Safe.

The word repeated itself over and over in my mind as we were funneled down the long, straight black line of the road. The glow of the headlights turned the empty sandlands into black walls. I smiled at the word sandlands. The brigadier would laugh and call it a neologism. We'd sit and have drinks, and the colonel would congratulate me on the size of the explosion. I would have to tell her I only called in the strike. I didn't make the bomb.

The blaring horn made me snap out of it. I swung the wheel right, and the huge truck screamed past, missing us by inches. Beverly opened her eyes and frowned.

"What was that?"

I smiled at her and reached for the flask of coffee. "Some fool who fell asleep at the wheel."

She sank back and closed her eyes again. "You OK?" She asked it as she drifted off.

"I'm fine," I told her. "Just fine."

I drove for another hour. The roads were long and very straight, and when I could see no lights ahead or behind us, I pushed the needle up as high as it would go, which was about one forty kilometers per hour, which was close to ninety. I had the window half-open so the cold desert air would batter my face. I kept going as long as I could, but fifteen miles outside Sirjan, I saw a gas station and pulled in. I figured we were about halfway to Bandar Abbas, which put it three or four hours away, and unless I got an hour's sleep, we would not make it because they'd be picking us out of the grill of a sixteen-wheeler with a pair of tweezers.

It was dark. I couldn't make out if the door and window on the shack were open or closed. It didn't look like a self-service kind of place. I figured there'd be some guy in dungarees and a straw hat out any moment to check the oil and wash the windshield. I'd ask him how far to Roswell, New Mexico, and he'd say "That *dee*-pends, Mr. Sir, on the gravity of your si-cher-ashon."

I snapped awake because somebody was knocking on the window. I took it in in a flash. There was a cop car parked over by the pumps twenty feet away. There was a cop standing by the window shining a flashlight at me as I lowered the window. There was another in back, shining a flashlight at the rear license plate.

The guy who'd knocked on the window said something to me in Persian. I mouthed and uttered noises like I had with the last cop, only worse, pointing at Beverly, who had not stirred. I figured she must be awake but thought it was smart to keep her eyes shut. The guy screwed up his face and shrugged and started raising his voice. I shrugged back, gesturing at Beverly again, "*Fansa ang. Fansa ang.*"

In the side mirror, I could see the guy in back hunkering down to look at the plates. "*Fansa ang,*" I said again, leaning back so he could see her. He leaned in, squinting, shining his flashlight on Beverly.

I was aware that it was important to spill no blood in the cab or on the truck. So the maneuver was tricky because I had to be quick. I'd pulled the Fairbairn and Sykes from my boot as I leaned back. Now I took hold of the back of his head with my left hand and slipped the blade in behind his left collarbone, driving it deep down into his heart, severing the aorta and the pulmonary artery. Death was pretty much instant.

I kept talking as I pushed the door open, making stupid grunting noises until he dropped and fell on his back. By this time, the other guy had come around with the detachable license plate in his hands. He gaped at me and frowned. He had a problem. He needed to let go of the plate before he could get his weapon. I already had the Maxim in my hand and put two slugs through his heart while he was still wondering what to do. I recovered my knife and put the plate back before filling up the tank and moving off. Beverly was either asleep or pretending to be asleep. I was awake now, wide awake, and figured I'd last another couple of hours.

What I didn't know was whether they had radioed in before knocking on the window. Had they figured they were going to give some guy a hard time for stopping with a girl by the side of the road? Or had they radioed dispatch that they were investigating suspicious behavior? There was no way of knowing. But I kept my eyes peeled for police activity.

For an hour, there was nothing. It was closing on five in the morning, and there was hardly a vehicle on the road. But as we passed the village of Qotobabad-e Kohareh, I saw a column of five military trucks moving north from where we had come. There were also a number of choppers. Most were military, but a couple were police, and they seemed to be scanning the desert.

The traffic began to pick up, and soon the horizon in the east started to turn pale. As we entered the town and turned onto the Emam Hosein Boulevard, I began to get glimpses of the sea far down on my left, and the sun began to bleed over the horizon. There was suddenly the noise and bustle of traffic, the honking of horns and the smell of gas fumes on the air. Beverly stirred, yawned and stretched, and pawed at the black cloth around her face.

I said, "Good morning."

She said, "My God..." She sat blinking for a moment and added, "Holy shit. What...? Where are we?"

"Bandar Abbas. From here, with just a little bit of luck, we get a boat."

"It happened," she said, half to herself. "All that happened."

"I'm afraid so."

As we got deeper into town, we began to see cafés and bakeries opening to the day. I lowered the window, and the smell of coffee was rich on the air. Finally we turned down a side street, and there, in front of us, was the blue expanse of the channel where the Persian Gulf meets the Gulf of Oman, and there, just three hundred yards away, on the other side of the road, was the marina.

I crossed the six lanes of traffic and pulled into the sprawling parking lot beside the marina. The lot was practically empty but for a cluster of cars parked in the shade of some trees that bisected the lot. I made for the far end, nearest the marina. I noticed as I went that practically every car I saw was a Peugeot. Others looked like Peugeot but had a badge that read IKCO. None of them was a filthy pickup. Lots of them were filthy, but not one of them was a pickup. I felt suddenly like a luminous inflatable condom at the vicar's tea party.

I pulled in beside a dumpster in the far corner of the lot, with the dumpster on my left and a line of cars on my right. I killed the engine and left the key in the ignition. I looked at Beverly for a moment, and she peered at me through the eye-slot in her burka.

"How are you feeling?"

She gave a small shrug. "Better. I slept a lot. I'm hungry."

"Good. Let's go get some coffee and breakfast at the marina."

I reached for the door, but she stopped me with an "Um..."

"What?"

"How do you eat and drink with one of these on?"

"I don't know. Maybe we could replace it with a scarf."

"Also, you look terrible. You look worse than terrible. You are a real mess. And I'm dressed in your clothes. We will draw attention."

I nodded. I reached for my cell and called the brigadier.

"Harry, I was about to call you. Where are you?"

"We're at Bandar Abbas, at the Haghani Marina parking

lot. We're in the only pickup truck in the lot. It's a beat-up blue Toyota. Have we got an extraction?"

He was silent for a moment. "Not exactly."

I tried to keep the anger out of my voice and failed. "What do you mean, not exactly, sir? We are five hundred and fifty miles from Kuwait, we have no money, and we will draw attention. We need to get out of here *now*."

"I know, Harry, and I am working flat-out to make that happen, but the nearest asset we had with access to a boat was in Tehran. He is on his way, but it could be several hours before he gets there."

"We won't be here in several hours."

"I know, Harry. Now listen very carefully. The US Carrier Strike Group 12 is in the area. My advice to you is do what you have to do to get to these coordinates."

I looked at my screen and saw Lat. 26°37′24.55″N— Long. 56°18′19.18″E.

"Where is that?"

"From where you are on the marina, you take a boat and sail in a perfectly straight line for thirty-five miles, past the island of Qeshm on your right and Larak on your left."

"*Thirty-five miles?*"

"You'll then be in Oman's territorial waters. There is a United States Navy vessel waiting for you there."

"But—"

"Harry." I stopped. "This is the situation, and we must deal with it. I have mobilized the US Navy to help you. You must do the rest. If you can steal a speedboat, you can make the rendezvous in half an hour or less."

"Yes, sir."

I hung up. Down in the marina, I could see maybe a couple

of dozen pleasure boats moored. There seemed to be free access to the piers, unlike Europe and the US, where they are fenced in and locked. That at least was something. But there were security guards. I counted four, and they were armed.

"Get in back and change into your own clothes," I told Beverly. "If you've got a scarf, put it over your head. If not, improvise something."

"What about you?"

I looked in the mirror and winced. "I'll wash my face and change my shirt."

She clambered in the back and pulled off the burka. I took it and ripped off a long strip. A quick glance told me there was nobody looking. I opened the gas tank and stuffed the strip of cloth inside, leaving a strip hanging out.

A moment later, Beverly climbed out of the truck looking almost normal with a scarf covering her head and partly hiding her face. I leaned in the back and changed my shirt for something that didn't look like I'd just escaped from a bloodbath and splashed some water on my face.

"OK," I told Beverly, "now we have to act fast." I rammed in the cigarette lighter, and while it was heating, I took the metal gas canisters from the back of the truck, opened them, and upended one on the ground and the other in the flatbed, spilling a good bit on the cloth I'd left dangling from the gas tank. I reached in the cab, grabbed the cigarette lighter, and told Beverly, "Start walking."

The gas was seeping away from the truck under the line of cars. I touched the lighter to the cloth. It flashed and started to burn. There was a big *whoosh!* and in seconds, the whole truck was burning. I grabbed Beverly's arm and hurried her toward the marina. Over my shoulder, I saw black smoke rising from the wheels of the Peugeot next to the truck.

We came level with a café facing the marina. There was a waiter serving a table with coffee and cakes. I shouted, pointing back toward the parking lot.

"*Atash! Atash! Dar Parking! Atash! Atash!*"

I was telling them there was fire in the parking lot. Beverly joined in, screaming like she was real worried, "*Atash dar Parking! Atash! Atash!*"

They were excitable. They all got up and ran to look, shouting at each other. The waiter ran inside, maybe to call the fire brigade or maybe just because he was so excited he needed to run somewhere.

We ran, too, down toward the security guards. There was a lot of black smoke billowing over the roof of the marina by now, and they had seen it, but we both shouted at them anyhow, pointing. "*Atash dar Parking! Atash! Atash!*"

At that point, my gas tank exploded, sending a fireball up into the air. The security guards started shouting at each other now, and pretty soon, they were running up toward the burning cars to see the fire.

We ran along to the next pier. There were four boats moored there. The farthest on the left, the *Shir Talayi*, looked fast, so I jumped aboard. I didn't need to tell her. Beverly was already releasing the mooring ropes. I took my Swiss Army knife, ripped out the ignition, and hotwired the engine. I put her in reverse, eased out, spun her around, and headed out of the harbor while black smoke billowed from the parking lot at the Haghani Marina in Bandar Abbas.

We described a big curve coming out of the harbor, set a bearing dead south, and gave it all she had over a flat sea under the rising sun. A mile out, doing close to seventy knots, we looked back. The smoke was billowing above the town, and flashing lights were just visible as the fire department arrived on the scene. There was no one following us. We gave each other big grins, and she flung her arms around me. And as I held her tightly with my right arm, I wiped away a tear with my left wrist.

"Damn sea wind," I said, and she laughed.

Twenty minutes later, the massive silhouette of the USS Abraham Lincoln Nimitz class aircraft carrier came into view, and five minutes after that, we left Iranian territorial waters, jumping and hooting for joy. I spun the wheel and headed aft of the carrier, where I could see a Liberty boat leaving the docking bay and heading out to meet us. We waved to them, and they waved back. I killed the motor, then turned to Beverly.

"We made it," I told her.

She nodded. "We made it."

And as we hugged tightly, I heard the voice over the megaphone. "*Ahoy! Shir Talayi! Prepare to be boarded!*"

I gave them the thumbs-up and told her, "You're going home, back to your dad."

EPILOGUE

IT WAS A MONTH LATER. I WAS SITTING ON A ROCK above Photographer's Point in the Wind River Mountains, gazing down to where Freemont Creek tumbles out of the Winds into a deep canyon on its long journey toward Freemont Lake. I told myself for the hundredth time as I sat there that there are no words in the human vocabulary to describe the view from up there. Even seeing it is not enough. You have to live it. It defies the weight of gravity and lifts your soul high above the hell that is this world and allows you to fly.

Before me, at my feet, I had the Carbine and the scope through which I had watched that massacre, back in Al-Landy, in Afghanistan, so long ago.

Miriam.

I smiled. I wondered how old she would be now if she had lived. Younger than Beverly. If she had lived—if Evil hadn't taken her. Evil with a capital E.

If ever I had doubted it in my youth, I now had absolute certainty that Evil was a living force that inhabited our world. I had seen it too many times, seen the unspeakable product of its intentions. I had looked into the darkness of its soul and knew it.

I hunkered down beside the hole I had dug and picked up the carbine and the scope, which I had wrapped in black silk. Then I lifted my gaze to the vast sweep of the clear blue sky.

"I don't know if you can hear me, Miriam, but I have carried you in my mind..." I hesitated and started again. "I have carried you in my heart for too many years, and maybe, I don't know, but maybe I have not let you rest." I shook my head. "I don't know if there is a God of Love and Kindness and Forgiveness. But if there is, I commit your soul to His care." I hesitated again, shrugged, and added, "Or her care, or their care. Whatever works. I guess if there is Evil in this world, there must be Goodness too. May it embrace you, Miriam, and keep you safe."

I laid the C8 Carbine and scope in their wooden cask in the hole I had dug, filled it in, tamped it down, and lay a large stone on top of it.

Then I sat a while, mourning a child I'd never had, who I'd named Miriam, mourning the childhood she might have had, the happiness she might have had, and the existence I might have had, devoted to life and love instead of death and vengeance.

Time to let go?

As long as Evil lived and thrived in our world, I could not let go.

Don't miss TIME TO DIE. The riveting sequel in the Harry Bauer Thriller series.

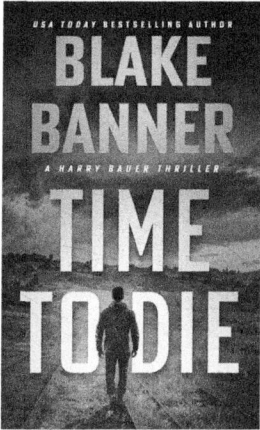

Scan the QR code below to purchase TIME TO DIE.

Or go to: righthouse.com/time-to-die

DON'T MISS ANYTHING!

If you want to stay up to date on all new releases in this series, with this author, or with any of our new deals, you can do so by joining our newsletters below.

In addition, you will immediately gain access to our entire *Right House VIP Library,* which includes many riveting Mystery and Thriller novels for your enjoyment!

righthouse.com/email

(Easy to unsubscribe. No spam. Ever.)

ALSO BY BLAKE BANNER

Up to date books can be found at:
www.righthouse.com/blake-banner

ROGUE THRILLERS
Gates of Hell (Book 1)
Hell's Fury (Book 2)
Ice Burn (Book 3)

ALEX MASON THRILLERS
Odin (Book 1)
Ice Cold Spy (Book 2)
Mason's Law (Book 3)
Assets and Liabilities (Book 4)
Russian Roulette (Book 5)
Executive Order (Book 6)
Dead Man Talking (Book 7)
All The King's Men (Book 8)
Flashpoint (Book 9)
Brotherhood of the Goat (Book 10)
Dead Hot (Book 11)
Blood on Megiddo (Book 12)
Son of Hell (Book 13)
Merchant of Death (Book 14)

HARRY BAUER THRILLER SERIES
Dead of Night (Book 1)
Dying Breath (Book 2)

The Einstaat Brief (Book 3)
Quantum Kill (Book 4)
Immortal Hate (Book 5)
The Silent Blade (Book 6)
LA: Wild Justice (Book 7)
Breath of Hell (Book 8)
Invisible Evil (Book 9)
The Shadow of Ukupacha (Book 10)
Sweet Razor Cut (Book 11)
Blood of the Innocent (Book 12)
Blood on Balthazar (Book 13)
Simple Kill (Book 14)
Riding The Devil (Book 15)
The Unavenged (Book 16)
The Devil's Vengeance (Book 17)
Bloody Retribution (Book 18)
Rogue Kill (Book 19)
Blood for Blood (Book 20)
The Cell (Book 21)
Time to Die (Book 22)

DEAD COLD MYSTERY SERIES
An Ace and a Pair (Book 1)
Two Bare Arms (Book 2)
Garden of the Damned (Book 3)
Let Us Prey (Book 4)
The Sins of the Father (Book 5)
Strange and Sinister Path (Book 6)
The Heart to Kill (Book 7)
Unnatural Murder (Book 8)
Fire from Heaven (Book 9)

ABOUT US

Right House is an independent publisher created by authors for readers. We specialize in Action, Thriller, Mystery, and Crime novels.

If you enjoyed this novel, then there is a good chance you will like what else we have to offer! Please stay up to date by using any of the links below.

Join our mailing lists to stay up to date -->
righthouse.com/email
Visit our website --> righthouse.com
Contact us --> contact@righthouse.com

facebook.com/righthousebooks
x.com/righthousebooks
instagram.com/righthousebooks

Printed in Great Britain
by Amazon